Tanner looked over at Bree. "You okay?"

She nodded. "Yeah, but let's get out of here. The turning-yourself-in plan doesn't seem like such a good one anymore."

A door clicked open at the other end of the hallway. Tanner grabbed Bree's hand and they ran in the opposite direction, barely making it around the corner without being seen.

Tanner didn't slow down.

They needed to get out of the building right now. But the only way to do that was to go back the way they came.

"We're trapped, aren't we?" she whispered. She dropped to the floor, opening her computer and resting it on her crossed legs. Within just a few seconds an alarm was going off at the front of the building.

"What is that?" he asked her.

She shrugged, getting up. "I triggered a window alarm near the northeast-side corner of the building. It won't buy us much time—"

He pulled her in for a quick, hard kiss. "But it will be enough."

SECURITY RISK

USA TODAY Bestselling Author

JANIE CROUCH

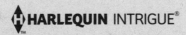

This book is dedicated to the ladies in the Crouch Crew. Thank you so much for all your support and encouragement. I couldn't do this without you!

ISBN-13: 978-1-335-60453-8

Security Risk

Copyright © 2019 by Janie Crouch

Recycling programs for this product may not exist in your area.

Printed in U.S.A.

www.Harlequin.com

Janie Crouch has loved to read romance her whole life. This *USA TODAY* bestselling author cut her teeth on Harlequin Romance novels as a preteen, then moved on to a passion for romantic suspense as an adult. Janie lives with her husband and four children overseas. She enjoys traveling, long-distance running, movie watching, knitting and adventure/obstacle racing. You can find out more about her at janiecrouch.com.

Books by Janie Crouch

Harlequin Intrigue

The Risk Series:
A Bree and Tanner Thriller

Calculated Risk
Security Risk

Omega Sector:
Under Siege

Daddy Defender
Protector's Instinct
Cease Fire
Major Crimes
Armed Response
In the Lawman's Protection

Omega Sector:
Critical Response

Special Forces Savior
Fully Committed
Armored Attraction
Man of Action
Overwhelming Force
Battle Tested

Omega Sector

Infiltration
Countermeasures
Untraceable
Leverage

Primal Instinct

Visit the Author Profile page at Harlequin.com.

CAST OF CHARACTERS

Tanner Dempsey—Deputy captain of the sheriff's office in Grand County, Colorado, who lives and works in Risk Peak.

Bree Daniels—Computer genius working as a waitress.

Alex Peterson and Nate Fletcher—Two cops killed in front of Tanner in an undercover mission three years ago.

Ryan Fletcher—Nate Fletcher's brother and district attorney in Denver.

Craig Michalski—Grand County psychiatrist who has been helping Tanner cope with his PTSD.

Blaine Duggan—Sheriff of Grand County.

Richard Whitaker—Deputy of the sheriff's office in Grand County.

Darin Carrico—Prison inmate about to be transferred from minimum security to maximum security and who hates all law enforcement.

Glen Carrico—Darin's brother, fighting to keep him from being transferred to maximum security.

Chapter One

The noose around his throat slowly strangled Tanner until gray blurred the edges of his vision. At the very last moment before he lost consciousness, he forced his weight onto his legs, providing blessed air. He knew the relief was short-lived. One leg was broken, the other almost useless after the hours of trying to support his weight on just his toes on the stool where he balanced precariously.

"Tell us who the cop is, and this can all end."

Tanner could barely see through his swollen eyes. "I already told you." The words were garbled whispers—blows to the face and the trauma to his throat had ensured that. "I'm the cop."

Someone pushed his leg out from under him, causing the rope to tighten around his neck once again, his hands tied behind his back rendering them useless. Airflow immediately ceased, although he didn't jerk or move unnecessarily. He'd learned after the first hour that flailing didn't accomplish anything but using up more energy and oxygen.

He had a limited supply of both.

"Which one of them is the cop? We know you were communicating with one of them."

The voice was referring to the two men also tied up with Tanner, but sitting in chairs, one barely twenty-one years old. Tanner couldn't see them. Couldn't hear them. Could only try to survive this moment.

Someone helped him plant his good leg back on the stool so he could relieve the tension on his throat. At least they'd finally figured out he couldn't talk while they were attempting to suffocate him.

He breathed in as much as his swollen throat would allow. "I wasn't communicating with one of them." That was the truth. He'd been communicating with both of them. All three of them had been sent undercover together. "It's just me."

The blow to his stomach caught him completely unaware and had him coughing up blood and struggling to balance on the stool. Tanner didn't know how much more he could take. But he would do whatever he had to if it meant Nate and Alex would walk out of here.

Tanner definitely wouldn't. He'd already made peace with that.

Before he could prep himself for another blow, someone ran into the opposite side of the warehouse screaming curses that would make a sailor proud.

"Cops! They're everywhere outside!"

For a split second Tanner felt hope. They were going to make it.

The hope died a moment later at the simple instructions the leader of the syndicate gave his men.

"Kill them all."

It echoed over and over in Tanner's head.

Kill them all.

Kill them all.

At the first blast of gunfire and thump of a body, Tanner used all his strength in one last Hail Mary attempt to dive from the stool. He could barely believe it when the rope gave way, snapping from the ceiling rather than ending his life. He crashed to the floor and—ignoring that agony lighting through his entire body—forced himself onto his feet.

And turned just in time to see one of the syndicate members point his Glock at twenty-one-year-old Nate Fletcher's forehead where he was strapped to a chair.

Tanner dived for them.

Eight hours later the nightmare still felt slick and slimy on Tanner Dempsey's skin. The flying motion had woken him up. It was what had woken him up, often violently, hundreds of nights since what happened in that warehouse three years ago.

Tanner was never in time to save Nate in his dream, just like he hadn't been in time to save him in real life. He'd watched as the life of a promising law enforcement officer—and human being—had been snuffed out.

Tanner had been too late to save Alex, the other undercover officer, too. He'd died with the first bullet when Tanner had still been strung up.

The place had been swarming with cops not a minute later. Almost everyone in the Viper Syndicate, a human- and weapons-trafficking cartel, had been caught or killed that day, too.

But not in time to save Nate or Alex.

Tanner scrubbed a hand over his face. He was sitting in a Denver courthouse, having finished giving his testimony in a drunk-driving case. Normally, he would've already left after providing his info, but he was staying to catch the prosecuting attorney during the court recess for lunch.

Ryan Fletcher, Nate's brother.

Maybe knowing he would be seeing Ryan today was what brought the nightmare back last night. Although, after three years' worth of required visits with the department psychiatrist, Tanner knew there didn't necessarily have to be a reason for his subconscious mind to start dwelling on what had happened that day. Sometimes his mind just went there of its own accord. Some PTSD triggers were visible, but many more were hidden.

He and Ryan had become not quite friends, but more than just professional colleagues over the last year since Ryan had moved to Colorado and become one of the district attorneys. When Tanner was in

Denver, or Ryan was in Grand County to see the sheriff, they sometimes got together to spar at the gym. Ryan might be a lawyer, but he kept himself in good shape.

And Tanner had worked damn hard to come back from what had happened at that warehouse. Tried to use his wounds—both physical and mental—to make him a better police officer. He demanded it of himself. As captain of the southeast department of the Grand County Sheriff's Office—which included his hometown of Risk Peak—he would do whatever it took to keep the people in his care safe.

A half smile popped up on his face before he could stop it. Risk Peak now included Bree Daniels, the woman who'd been causing smiles to pop up on his face unbidden for months.

She'd run out of money, and hope, in Risk Peak three months ago while being chased by a terrorist organization. Normally, Tanner wasn't thankful for bad guys, but the fact that these had led the socially awkward yet breathtakingly beautiful Bree to his front door was enough for him to make an exception.

"We haven't won the case yet." Ryan walked up to him and slapped him on the shoulder. "You might want to save grinning like an idiot for when we do."

Tanner reached out to shake the man's hand. "Think there's going to be any problem getting a conviction?"

"That would be a definite no. Guy was on a suspended license and ran from the police. Plus, I've got

Dr. Michalski providing his professional evaluation of the defendant this afternoon."

Tanner nodded. "Dr. Michalski is good." Tanner should know—he'd been seeing the man for three years. Tanner wasn't a huge fan of his sessions—sometimes it felt like he had a million other things to do than just sit around and talk about the past, but he couldn't deny that Dr. Michalski was a good psychiatrist.

"Yeah, he's definitely better on the stand than the last department psychiatrist I worked with in Seattle. Jury responds much better to him." Ryan grinned. "Of course, he's never going to be as good as putting you on the stand. Anytime I know you'll be testifying, I try to get as many women in the jury as possible."

Tanner rolled his eyes. He'd been teased about his looks before, by both the district attorneys and his colleagues in the sheriff's department. But as far as he was concerned, there was only one person whose opinion of his looks mattered. And it definitely wasn't anybody in a jury.

"Anything I can do to help get bad guys off the street."

"Speaking of." Ryan's easy smile slid from his face. "You heard that Owen Duquette got released on parole last week?"

Tanner swallowed a curse and nodded. "I made my objections known to the parole board. Strongly. Both in written form and in person at the parole hearing."

"It just feels like a slap in the face, you know? Duquette might not have been in the warehouse that day, but he knew what was going on. He was complicit in Nate's death. I'm sure of it." Ryan's fist tightened around his briefcase handle.

But they both knew that knowing something and *proving* it in court were two entirely different things. Duquette's ties to the Viper Syndicate had been tentative at best, legally. The district attorney at the time had only been able to charge Duquette with relatively minor trafficking charges, not murder.

But still, to get out after only three years? Tanner was angry. He couldn't even imagine how Ryan felt, knowing someone they both highly suspected was connected to his brother's murder was now back out on the streets.

"I'll make it my business to keep an eye on him," Tanner said. "And not just while I'm in uniform. The second he steps out of line, I'll make sure he goes down."

Ryan nodded. "Thanks. It's just…you know. Nate would've been twenty-five this month."

Tanner had to look away. If he had just snapped that rope a few seconds earlier, maybe Nate would've been here.

But that was Tanner's burden to bear. "Duquette will get what's coming to him. Don't doubt it."

A career criminal like Duquette wouldn't stay on the straight and narrow very long. Tanner would use whatever resources he had to know the moment Duquette stepped in the wrong direction.

Ryan nodded, then looked over Tanner's shoulder. "Oh, hi, Dr. Michalski. Got a moment to go over a couple of last-minute details?"

"Sure, Ryan." Dr. Michalski stepped up beside Tanner and offered his hand to shake. "Tanner, good to see you. It's been a while."

Translation: *You missed your last required appointment.*

Response: *Sorry, it just happened to be scheduled when I was off saving the country from a terrorist group about to illegally access cell-phone data all over the world.*

Neither man actually said it.

"Doc. Good to see you, too."

"Everything okay? No anger…problems?"

The good doctor had obviously heard Tanner's discussion about Duquette.

"Yeah, I'm fine. Just a little frustrated when my job gets harder because of criminals getting released early."

"Maybe we can talk about that sometime."

Tanner resisted the urge to roll his eyes. "Sounds like a plan. I'll let you guys get to your discussion."

Ryan smiled. "Tanner, thanks again for your work on the stand. Stellar, as always. Next time bring a cowboy hat in case we need an extra push with the lady jurors."

Tanner shook hands with both men before saying his goodbyes.

Because there was someone else he knew for a fact found him attractive in a cowboy hat. Someone who barely came up to his chin and had waves of thick brown hair running down her back. Someone to whom it never occurred to wear makeup, but it didn't matter because her natural beauty could give a cover model a run for their money any day of the week.

One look into her green eyes would have him forgetting about psychiatrists, witness stands and even the ghostly itch of a noose stretched around his neck.

Chapter Two

He watched Tanner Dempsey leave the courthouse just like he'd watched him all day. He'd silently observed, no one discovering what he was really doing. What he was really planning.

Had Dempsey realized he was watching? Of course not. Because Tanner Dempsey was so full of himself he couldn't possibly conceive that someone might watch him with contempt or scorn or disdain.

The handsome cop with the charming smile couldn't possibly devise that someone didn't fall under the spell of his charisma.

The man felt bile churning in his stomach as he saw how friendly other people were with Dempsey. It was impossible to understand how everyone surrounding the cop in the courthouse wasn't sickened by his arrogance. How he obviously thought himself better than everyone.

And then people shook his hand, smiling and friendly. Fooled. They couldn't see the truth right in front of them—that Dempsey was fooling them all.

It had taken every ounce of restraint the man had to not stand up in the courtroom and scream out that Dempsey was a fraud.

Dempsey thought the rules did not apply to him. Thought he could just do whatever he wanted. That everyone he arrested and testified against was no better than a bug beneath his shoe.

But soon they would all learn the truth about Tanner Dempsey's conceit. He would get what was coming to him.

It was time for the lawman to fall from grace. And the man would make sure that happened.

Chapter Three

"Order up, Bree!"

Bree Daniels smiled at Gayle Little sitting at the table in front of her. "So then what did Mr. Little do?"

Mrs. Little frowned. "Dan just yelled for you. Don't you need to go get the food?"

Bree smiled gently at the older woman. Mrs. Little came in a few times a week since her husband of sixty years had passed away recently. Bree knew Dan would much rather Bree stay out here and talk to Mrs. Little—to listen to her tell a story Bree had already heard—than to rush back and get the food.

"Don't you worry about Dan. He'll take the food out himself if I don't get back there in time."

There would've been a point not long ago that Bree wouldn't have realized that staying and talking to Mrs. Little was more important than getting the food from the kitchen. She wouldn't have realized there wasn't a single customer in the Sunrise Diner who wouldn't gladly eat a lukewarm meal if it meant seeing Mrs. Little—a woman most of them had known all their lives—forget her sadness for a spell.

It had only been over the last few weeks of living here in Risk Peak that Bree had begun to understand the nuances of interacting with people. It wasn't something that came easily for her.

She was probably the only genius-level hacker in the world working at a mom-and-pop diner in the middle of nowhere, without a computer in sight. Most people would say it was a waste of her talent, but Bree didn't care. If she never saw another computer, that would be just fine with her.

Computers, and her talent with them, had gotten her tortured as a child, gotten her mother killed and had nearly cost her her life a few months ago. So working as a waitress was just fine with her.

"And then he surprised me by getting down on one knee right then and there and asking me to marry him. On our third date," Mrs. Little said, a dreamy look in her eyes.

Bree's smile was genuine, feeling no urge to tell the older woman she'd heard the story before. It was so sweet and romantic.

At least she no longer sat tensely through every conversation worried that however she responded would be wrong or inappropriate.

While Bree didn't miss working with computers, she had to admit she found them much more simple than people. Coding held no subtext—it was straightforward, inputs and outputs, and for Bree as basic and simple as breathing.

Relationships and people, on the other hand? They were the opposite: full of unspoken rules and expectations and subtext.

Simple things other people took for granted, like talking and joking and, heaven forbid, *flirting*, were causes of darn near panic attacks in Bree. Part of it was from growing up without any friends and a mother terrified they'd be taken back into captivity at any moment. The other part of it was just how Bree's brain worked.

Like a computer.

Mrs. Little patted Bree's hand as she finished her story, and Bree turned back toward the kitchen. Sure enough, someone had already taken the food out to the table where it belonged.

For just a moment she tensed, second-guessing herself and whether she'd made the wrong decision by talking to Mrs. Little rather than concentrating on the job she was being paid to do. But both Dan and Cheryl smiled at her when she turned back toward the kitchen, so Bree decided not to worry about it.

She had bigger things to worry about. Tanner was on his way to come get her. Said he had a surprise for her this evening.

Bree did not do well with surprises.

She knew he'd been in Denver today providing testimony in court. The fact that she couldn't call him and ask him for more details about this evening had just ratcheted up her anxiety.

What did it mean when a man said he had a surprise, but that it wasn't a date and that she should definitely not get dressed up?

What did that *mean*?

"You okay, honey?" Cheryl came and stood beside her and rubbed her arm.

Not too long ago that sort of casual touch would've been completely foreign to Bree. Living a lifetime without anyone touching her had made all touches feel odd.

Judy, the other full-time waitress, came and flanked Bree on the other side, knocking Bree's hip with her own.

"You've been staring at that pitcher of tea for a full minute. You thinking about asking it out on a date? Tanner would probably be jealous."

The sound of his name just made her abdomen muscles tighten more.

"I'm scared," she finally whispered.

Saying it, talking personally about herself, was still so difficult. But these women were her friends.

Friends. Still such a foreign concept.

Both women immediately pulled in closer. Cheryl wrapped her arm around Bree's waist. "Scared of what, honey? Do you feel like someone is watching you again? Do you think it's the Organization?"

"They're gone," Judy assured her. "They may not be in prison yet, but none of them are free. Espe-

cially not Michael Jeter. He's not going to get anywhere near you."

Bree shuddered at the name of the man who'd
kept her and her mother captive and hurt them both
to force Bree to use her computer talents to further
his agenda. Her mother had never fully recovered
from his torture. But they were right—Jeter was currently awaiting trial and couldn't hurt her anymore.

"No, not Jeter," she whispered. "Tanner."

"You're afraid of *Tanner*?" Judy asked.

This was why Bree didn't like talking. She always messed it up. She could feel herself withdrawing, falling back into old, bad patterns of retreat that
were more familiar.

But Cheryl got right up in Bree's face. "Hey. Talk
to us."

Bree looked in the older woman's eyes. There was
no judgment there, just acceptance and kindness.

"Order up," Dan yelled from the kitchen window
a few feet away.

"In a minute!" both Cheryl and Judy responded
in sync. Dan sighed.

"Why would you be scared of Tanner? Did something happen?" Judy asked.

Spitting it out was probably the best option. "He's
coming to get me in an hour. Said he had a surprise
and not to get dressed up."

"A surprise isn't bad, Bree." Cheryl rubbed her
arm again. "Granted, that boy should know better

than to think you're going to like surprises, but it's definitely not something to be afraid about."

"But he told me not to get dressed up! That means he doesn't want me to go to any trouble with my hair and makeup if he's just going to tell me it's over."

The other two women met each other's eyes.

"Or…" Judy drew the word out. "He has something else planned and he doesn't want you to worry about a dress or fancy shoes."

Bree's forehead wrinkled as she considered that. "Like what?"

"I've got another order up, gals," Dan said from the window again.

"In a minute!" Now Bree joined the battle cry. She looked to her friends with a little more hope.

"Maybe a hike," Judy said. "I know it's colder out, but you both like to hike."

Cheryl took the pitcher of tea from Bree's hands and set it down on the counter. "Maybe stargazing. That's romantic. He wouldn't want you to get dressed up for that."

Judy gave a one-shouldered shrug. "A motorcycle ride. I know he doesn't have one, but maybe he borrowed one."

"The point is, the words *surprise* and *casual* are not bad. Tanner Dempsey is nothing if not straightforward. That man is never going to blindside you." Cheryl kissed her on the cheek, and then both women smiled and headed toward the kitchen to keep Dan from having a fit with undelivered food.

Bree turned and made her way back over to Mrs. Little, pouring her some more tea.

She wasn't convinced surprises weren't bad. She'd had a lot of years where the unknown meant dangerous or painful.

But one thing they said was definitely true: Tanner wouldn't blindside her.

He'd spent the last month helping her with damn near everything. Helping her move back into the Andrewses' small apartment on the outskirts of town. Helping her learn how to interact with others. Helping her figure out how to navigate her life now that she wasn't on the run anymore.

And most important, helping her deal with the crippling loss of the twins she no longer had to care for. She knew Christian and Beth were back where they belonged, in their mother's—Bree's cousin Melissa's—care. But after nearly three months of being their sole caretaker, losing them so suddenly had left a huge gap in Bree's life.

Tanner had distracted her with dates and horse-back rides at his ranch and kisses that curled her toes.

So Judy and Cheryl were right. Bree wasn't exactly sure where her relationship with him was going, but if he had something bad to say, he wouldn't beat around the bush.

The door to the diner chimed as it opened, and as if her thoughts had conjured him, Tanner was there—all long legs and big, broad shoulders that almost filled the door before he made his way inside.

Her gaze continued up to his face, his thick dark hair cut short. That square jaw covered in what seemed to be an almost perpetual five o'clock shadow.

Those brown eyes.

Bree couldn't stop staring. Even knowing she was standing there holding a pitcher of tea in the middle of a restaurant and just *staring*, she still couldn't stop.

But at least he was staring at her, too.

He closed the distance between them, stopping when he was a few feet from her. "I know I'm early. I just had to see you. Today has been…"

She took a step closer. "Are you okay? Did anything happen?"

Every single part of her body seemed to clench as he reached out and trailed his thumb down her cheek. "It's all fine now."

She couldn't look away from those brown eyes. It wasn't so long ago that she found it hard to look him in the eyes, but more often than not now she found it impossible to look away. "Fine. I mean, good. I'm glad it's fine."

He took her awkwardness in stride as always. "I'll just sit out here until you're finished and chat with Dan and folk, if that's okay."

Sure. The word formed in her brain, but she couldn't seem to get it out of her mouth as his thumb trailed down her cheek again. She nodded abruptly then turned away, almost running back toward the kitchen.

Judy and Cheryl were both grinning like idiots.

"Yeah, I'm definitely going to go with 'not a bad surprise' for my final answer," Judy said.

Cheryl turned Bree around so Bree's back was to her.

"What are you doing?" Bree said as she felt the knot of her apron loosen.

"Dan's basically been running the whole restaurant by himself for the last half hour anyway. We don't need you here." Cheryl pushed her gently between the shoulder blades back toward the front of the restaurant. "You've got a gorgeous man out there who couldn't bear to wait one more hour to see you. Go get changed out of your work clothes. Whatever his surprise is, you want it."

Chapter Four

It didn't take Bree long to figure out where they were going, and the last of her tension eased away. He was taking her to her favorite place on the planet: the ranch Tanner shared with his brother, Noah, about thirty minutes outside Risk Peak.

She'd stayed here when she'd been on the run, and it was impossible not to fall in love with this place. Horses and quiet and mountains. No people ever around except for Noah, who rarely made his presence known at all.

She and Tanner usually came here on the weekends. He'd taught her how to ride and care for the horses. But they'd never come in the evening.

Her heart clenched a little as he led her around the house. Of all her memories of the twins, waking up and seeing them both outside in Tanner's big, capable arms as he walked and showed them the horses was forever ingrained in her psyche.

"Hey, what's that sad look for?"

She gave a one-shouldered shrug. "Just… Beth and Christian. I miss them."

"Have you Skyped this week?" He took her hand, his long fingers stretching securely over hers.

She nodded. "Of course. Melissa and Chris know if they don't call me as scheduled, I'll never let them hear the end of it. But it's just not the same." She couldn't help her little sigh. "They're happy and safe and together as a family, and I want that for them."

"But you miss them."

"Crazy, right? They were never mine to begin with." She'd tried to warn herself of that, but those babies had stolen her heart.

"Not crazy at all. But maybe my surprise will help make it better." He led her over to his barn.

"Did you guys get a new horse?" Now, that would be a wonderful surprise. Bree loved interacting with all the animals here, since she'd never had any sort of pet growing up.

"Better." He took her hand and pulled her toward a stall in the far corner.

She rounded the doorway so she could see and couldn't stop her near squeal of pleasure. "Corfu had her puppies!"

"And one is yours, if you want it."

"Really?" It was all she could do not to jump up and down and clap her hands. She knew she was acting like an idiot but couldn't help it.

A puppy.

It wouldn't be the same as having the twins, but it would be a *puppy*. And it would be hers.

Tanner took her hand and led her closer to Corfu—a mixed-breed dog who'd just shown up on the ranch a year ago. "They're nearly a week old already, since Noah didn't see fit to mention the fact that Corfu had given birth to me until yesterday."

The four pups were lying snuggled next to Corfu, who lifted her head and sniffed at Bree as Bree crouched beside her.

"Is it okay to pet her?"

Tanner crouched down, too. "Sure. She knows you're her friend."

Bree scratched the dog's head gently, smiling as she leaned into Bree's fingers.

"They're so little!" She touched one gently. "Which one is mine?"

"There are three boys and one girl. You'll have to decide."

"Boy," she said instantly. "I want that one. I'll name him Star." She pointed to the one in the middle—black, with a large white spot on its head.

Tanner laughed softly and scooped the puppy up. "I'm afraid you'll have to make a tough decision."

"Is he already spoken for?" It was ridiculous to be disappointed. Any puppy would be great.

"No, you just can't have a boy pup *and* this one. Star is a girl." He held the pup out to her.

"A girl," Bree breathed then smiled, taking the

tiny pup in her arms. "Of course you're a girl. You're a beautiful, sweet girl, and we'll be best friends."

They played with the pups a few more minutes before Tanner said they should let Corfu and the babies rest.

"I can't take her with me tonight?" The thought of having the pup around in her apartment that always seemed too quiet was so appealing.

Tanner slipped an arm around her shoulders and pulled her close as they walked out of the barn and toward his house. "It'll be another five weeks before she's weaned. No sleepovers until then."

Five weeks wasn't that long. Hell, before a couple of months ago, she'd spent years without talking to anyone or having any human contact. Surely she could survive a little over a month without a dog.

He spun her around to face him as they got to his house. "It's been harder than you've let on, hasn't it? Being by yourself."

She shrugged. She didn't want to be a whiner. "I was by myself for a lot of years, even before my mother died. Seems silly to complain about it now when I'm finally *not* alone."

He took a step closer, his hands dropping to her waist. "I know I'm not as cute as those twins, but you really aren't alone. I'm always here if you need me." His forehead dropped against hers. "Okay?"

She couldn't worry about anything when Tanner

was this close. All she could do was breathe in the scent of him, woodsy and fresh and undeniably male.

She rose up onto her toes when his lips moved toward hers. Her mind might work like a computer, but her body was all woman when she was around him. She shivered as his thumb brushed over her jaw, then felt like she was melting out of her own skin as he kissed the side of her mouth before running his tongue over her lower lip.

He kissed her gently like that until she couldn't stand it anymore and she threaded her hands into his hair at his nape and pulled him hard against her. She gasped as the pleasure radiated through her, heard him groan and knew he was feeling the same. They both surrendered to the heat between them, lost in sensation.

When they finally broke away, both of them were breathing hard. His forehead fell against hers again. "I think I better get you home."

She wanted to ask him to stay with her tonight. To take that next step their kisses had been moving them toward for the last few weeks. Every time they were pressed up together, it was abundantly clear he wanted her. If she gave him the go-ahead, would he make that next move? Would he finally give her whatever it was her body needed to ease the restlessness and heat that seemed to thrum through her every time he was around?

If he were just waiting on her, she'd tell him she

was ready right now, this very moment. She might not have experienced sex before, but she wasn't afraid. Not with Tanner. He wouldn't hurt her. She knew that more than anything else.

But it was more than just her own natural hesitation. Something was holding him back, too. Something she was too bad at interpreting interpersonal cues to figure out. He never made her think it had anything to do with her. But still...

She was missing a lot of the emotional components other women—*normal* women—weren't. Women who hadn't been born with a brain that worked like a computer and sentiment that sometimes didn't seem to work at all. Women who hadn't had to shut down emotionally because they'd been tortured. Women who hadn't been on the run for half their life with no interaction with other people.

All those things left some pretty large gaps in Bree's emotional development. Maybe subconsciously Tanner was realizing Bree wouldn't be able to provide all he would need, and he wanted to keep from taking that last physical step that would make it harder for them to break apart if they needed to.

Why else would he be stopping, when his body still pressed up against hers made it clear he wanted her? At least physically.

"Let's get you home," he whispered.

The ride back to Risk Peak was mostly in silence, but not uncomfortable. Tanner's hand never left hers, bringing her fingers up to his lips to kiss every so often.

It just made Bree more confused. The urge to blurt out all her questions was overwhelming, and a few months ago she wouldn't have been able to stop herself. But she forced herself to remain quiet rather than demand answers for things that didn't make sense to her.

The fact that there were more kisses after he parked at her apartment on the outskirts of town, and the fact that her body was fairly humming by the time they pulled away from each other, didn't help with her confusion.

He took the key she offered and unlocked the door, checking her apartment for any threats before letting her inside. He always did that, even though there hadn't been any sign of trouble since they'd disbanded the Organization almost two months ago. But she didn't mind him doing it. The fact that he put himself between her and any potential danger made her feel cherished.

He kissed her forehead. "I'll see you tomorrow?"

Stay.

She screamed at herself to say it. To just tell him outright that she was ready. That she wanted him. Wanted *this*.

But before she got up the nerve, with one more kiss to her forehead, Tanner was gone.

She sighed and called herself every type of idiot

for not voicing her desires. How was it she couldn't seem to get herself to *shut up* when she was blurting out something inappropriate for a situation, and now couldn't seem to force herself to *speak up* when there was something legitimately good she wanted?

She eventually got ready for bed, but once she was there, she couldn't sleep. After thirty minutes she gave up even trying. She couldn't do anything about Tanner, but she could research puppies.

Maybe that would take her mind off everything else.

She went over to her desk, running her fingers across her laptop. Even opening it caused her to tense, but researching something as innocent and fun as this didn't need to bring back any of the bad memories.

Once she got started, habit took over, and all discomfort from using a computer was left behind. Within an hour she had read multiple articles on canine physical, mental and emotional development. Then she researched and made a list of everything she would need to buy the next time she was in Denver. It was probably a good thing she had five weeks before Star could come home; there were a lot of things a puppy needed. She wouldn't be caught off guard this time, like she had been when the twins had been thrust into her care.

She was still wide awake when she got to the recommended square footage of outdoor space a dog that size would require. She had a small plot of backyard, which would need a fence. She would have to talk to Dan and Cheryl about that. But more important, would it even be big enough to meet the recommended size? Would she still be allowed to get the dog if it wasn't?

Knowing her brain would never let her sleep until she knew the exact square footage in her backyard, Bree slipped on a pair of sweatpants with her sleep shirt and some shoes. Grabbing a tape measure and her phone so she could type in the measurements, she headed outside.

She was glad she didn't have any neighbors around to see her out measuring her yard in the middle of the night. Using the tape measure, she began marking off quadrants, typing them into her phone as she went. She was at the farthest point from the apartment when she took a step backward and tripped over something.

Cursing, she slid back, turning on the flashlight on her phone so she could see what had tripped her. She didn't remember there being any logs or large rocks in her yard. Although they weren't necessarily bad—a dog might like them.

But when she shone the light, she realized it wasn't a log at all. She'd tripped over a *person*. She couldn't see the face of the person passed out facedown, but it looked like a man by the size of him.

"Hey, are you okay?" she said. She poked his shoulder when he didn't respond. "Excuse me. Wake up."

When he didn't move at all, fear began to crawl

along her belly. She reached over to take the guy's pulse.

His skin was cold to the touch, and there was definitely no pulse to be found.

She hadn't just tripped over a person. She'd tripped over a *body*.

Chapter Five

Tanner groped for the phone, his mind becoming instantly alert as it rang on his bedside table. After ten years in law enforcement, he'd gotten used to having it go off at any and all hours of the day or night.

But when he saw it was Bree, his heart began to gallop. She wouldn't call at four o'clock in the morning without reason.

"Bree, what's wrong?"

Her breath sawing in and out didn't ease his fear in any way. He was already getting out of bed and putting on his clothes. "Bree? Talk to me, freckles."

"Tanner? There's a…body."

He cursed as he zipped and buttoned his jeans. "Are you okay? Are you hurt?"

"No. I'm not hurt."

He pulled on a shirt and began buttoning it. "But someone was inside your apartment?"

"No, I found the body outside."

He had no idea why she would've found a body outside in the middle of the night. Maybe someone was drunk and passed out on her lawn. Maybe it wasn't a body at all.

"Are you inside? Safe?"

"Y-yes." The barely whispered word didn't reassure him.

"Just stay where you are, okay? Don't move. I'm at my place in town. I'll be to you in less than five minutes."

He hated to hang up but had to so he could call the station and get Ronnie Kitchens, the deputy on duty tonight, out to the scene. Tanner would meet them there. He was pulling up to Bree's place by the time he got off the phone with Ronnie.

Weapon drawn, he approached her front door, keeping an eye out all around him.

He knocked. "Bree, open up, sweetheart. It's me." He kept his eyes pinned out in the darkness, looking for any sign of movement.

The door creaked open just slightly. "Tanner?"

He hated to hear the fear in her voice, so much more noticeable because it had been conspicuously absent for the last month. "Yeah, freckles. Let me in, okay?"

The door opened wider, and he stepped inside, holstering his weapon and pulling her against him in a one-armed hug. "Are you all right?" He looked around the room. Nothing seemed out of place or destroyed.

"Yes, i-it's out back. Outside. I tripped over it." A shudder racked her small frame.

"I want you to stay here. Ronnie will be here in just a minute, and we're going to check it out." He led her to the kitchen table and helped her sit in a chair. "Why were you outside in the middle of the night?"

"I was measuring the yard to see if it was regulation size for a dog."

Even with the gravity of the situation, Tanner almost smiled. Measuring a yard in the middle of the night for her new puppy? That totally made sense in a Bree world.

"Sweetheart, not that I doubt you, but are you sure it was a body?"

"Yes. I tried to get him to move before I called you. In case it was someone who'd fallen asleep or something."

That didn't sound good.

"Okay." He rubbed his hand soothingly over her hair. "Stay here. I'm going to check it out."

The lights from Ronnie's squad car were reflecting in the windows, so Tanner went outside to meet him.

"We definitely have a body?" Ronnie asked as he exited his car, a little slower than he'd once been after narrowly escaping a body bag himself a few weeks ago.

"Bree says it's out back. I haven't confirmed. Said she tripped over it when she was measuring the yard for her new dog."

Ronnie stopped and stared at him. "Do I even

want to ask why she would be doing that in the middle of the night?"

Tanner shrugged. "It's Bree. Once she gets her brain set on something, there's no way around it."

The whole town was getting used to that response. Ronnie was no exception. "Let's go check it out."

They grabbed high-powered flashlights from the squad car and moved quickly to the back of the house, firearms once again drawn. Bree's patch of land wasn't that large, and it didn't take them long to realize Bree hadn't been mistaken.

There was very definitely a dead body.

Ronnie muttered a curse and kept him covered with his weapon as Tanner rushed over. As soon as he touched the cold skin of the male body lying on his stomach, Tanner knew there was no way the guy was alive. But he checked the pulse anyway.

Dead.

"We need to get the crime lab out here. Definitely dead—for a while, it feels like." Tanner stood, backing away from the body to try to keep the scene as pristine as possible.

"Natural causes?" Ronnie asked.

Tanner shone his light on the back of the guy's shirt. It was covered with blood. "Nope. Nothing natural about this."

TANNER STAYED OUTSIDE as forensics made their way onto the scene and began processing, using the floodlights they brought. It didn't take long to realize the guy not only hadn't died of natural causes, he'd been murdered. The multiple stab wounds covering his back were testament to that.

Tanner kept Bree inside the house. She was curious, but coming face-to-face with this sort of violence under the glaring lights wasn't something he'd suggest for anyone. Not to mention it was now an active crime scene that shouldn't be contaminated.

It wasn't long before he was having to give that excuse to more than just Bree. The lights had woken folks up, and before long there were curious bystanders from all over town stopping by. It wasn't every day someone was murdered in Risk Peak.

Ronnie was doing his best to shoo them along, thankfully having set up the crime scene tape far enough back to keep this from becoming an online media sensation.

"Captain Dempsey." Owen, one of the crime lab techs, jogged over to him. "We've done all our preliminary processing and are ready to turn the body over."

Time to find out if they had a dead local on their hands. Tanner prayed he wouldn't be making a dreaded trip to the house of someone he knew to tell them a loved one had been killed.

He and Ronnie both joined the two techs as they reached down and rolled over the body. Ronnie let out a relieved breath. "That's nobody from Risk Peak, right? Thank God."

Relief flooded Tanner, too. "Yeah, I think you're right. I don't recognize—"

Tanner stopped. Because he *did* recognize the dead man, although it wasn't someone from here. He let out a blistering curse.

"What?" Ronnie asked. "Is it someone we know?"

Tanner crouched down beside the body. "Someone *I* know. Joshua Newkirk. He was arrested four years ago, and then he got out on early release six months ago. He's from farther north in Grand County. Raped a woman there. I was part of the team who arrested him."

And now, four years later, he was out and might have been on his way to attack Bree. The MO was similar. Newkirk had broken into the other woman's house while she was alone.

Tanner stood back up. "Damn it, I told the parole board he should be kept in prison. That the risk of repeat offense was too high."

Just like he'd said about Owen Duquette earlier today. Different parole board, same situation. It was hard to keep the community safe if they were going to continue letting offenders back onto the streets so soon.

Ronnie stepped back so the crime lab could continue their job. "Well, he won't be attacking any more women now, that's for sure."

Tanner shook his head. "I can't even pretend I'm going to lose sleep over Newkirk's death." Damn well not, since they'd found the man on Bree's lawn.

"That didn't give someone the right to kill him." Ronnie shook his head.

Tanner scrubbed a hand over his face. "No, of course not. We'll bring that person to justice. But damn it, Ronnie, the guy was twenty feet from Bree's door."

Owen the crime tech looked up. "I don't think this guy was planning to attack the lady who lives here."

Tanner focused in on Owen. "Why?"

"I don't know if this is going to make it better or worse, but this guy wasn't killed here. There would've been a crap ton of blood."

Ronnie raised an eyebrow. "Crap ton? That a clinical term?"

"I'm just saying that if this guy was stabbed here, there would be blood pooling around him."

Tanner looked around. He didn't see any blood, either. "What does that mean, exactly?"

"One option is that guy could've been stabbed closer to town and just made it this far before giving up the ghost, pardon the pun. We'll look for blood traces and see if we can follow it anywhere. Might get lucky and lead us to the actual murder scene."

"That would be highly useful. But there's another option?" Tanner asked.

Owen's brows furrowed. "Well, the body could've been placed here. Unless we find some sort of blood trace leading from somewhere, then I would assume that the body was dumped here by the killer."

Damn it, that was almost as bad as thinking a

rapist had been on his way to Bree's house. "Why would someone dump a body here?" Tanner barked. "Specifically at this apartment?"

Owen shrugged. "That I can't tell you. Maybe because it's pretty far at the edge of town and this just happened to be a convenient place, but..." He trailed off.

He wasn't going to like what Owen was going to say, but the younger man still needed to say it. "You can tell me, Owen. I'm not going to kill the messenger."

"You only dump a body in someone's yard if you want it to be found. Otherwise, there's ten thousand acres of national forests all around us. Why not drag it in there and leave it? Could be years before anyone found him."

"So it was some sort of message to her?" Ronnie asked. "Does she have any connection to Joshua Newkirk?"

Tanner shook his head. "I've got no reason to think so, but I'll ask."

"For what it's worth—" Owen crouched down next to the body again "—it's a lot more likely that this has nothing to do with her. Somebody could've killed Newkirk and just decided to dump the body here before going any farther. Like I said, her apartment is on the edge of town, so dumping it here, in the dark, makes sense. I'll know more in a few hours."

Tanner and Ronnie stepped back farther so he

could go to work. Ronnie slapped Tanner on the shoulder. "We'll get answers."

Tanner nodded. "I'll ask Bree if she knew Newkirk."

He turned back toward the house and found Bree standing in her back door, fully dressed but still with a blanket wrapped around her as if to ward off a chill. And who could blame her? There was a dead rapist a couple dozen feet from her house.

Tanner walked up to Bree. God, he hated that pinched look that was back on her features. It had been there so much when he'd first met her but had been gone for a while.

He wanted it gone again.

"Was it someone from around here? Someone we know?" she asked.

Tanner wrapped his arms around her. "No, freckles. Not anyone from around here." He could feel some of the tension leak out of her. "Do you know someone named Joshua Newkirk?"

She pulled back so she could look him in the eye. "No. Should I?"

He believed her. She had no reason to lie about it, and he didn't think Bree was very good at lying anyway.

"That's the dead guy's name. I was able to ID him pretty quickly because I arrested him a few years ago. Evidently, he's made a few enemies since getting out of prison six months ago."

And while Tanner was grateful a rapist hadn't been on his way up to Bree's back door, he didn't like how any of this was feeling to him.

He prayed Owen's last statement would be correct, and that Bree's yard had just been a convenience. That it was just a coincidence that the body had been placed here.

Tanner wasn't prone to believing in coincidences. Anger and frustration pooled inside him. She'd been through enough. He'd brought her to Risk Peak to keep her safe, and now this. The worst could've happened, and he wouldn't have been able to prevent it.

He felt her small hands close over his fists.

"I'm okay. Whatever's going on in that head of yours didn't happen. You'll figure out what's going on and put a stop to it. Give yourself time."

The trust in her eyes gutted him. He stroked his knuckles down her cheek. There were so many things he wanted to say to her, to assure her of, but the phone rang in his pocket. He grabbed it and saw it was Sheriff Duggan, his boss.

Bree waved at him to get it and turned and walked toward her bedroom.

"Sheriff Duggan."

"I hear there's a body in Bree Daniels's yard."

Tanner wasn't surprised word had already reached her. Grand County wasn't big enough that a murder wouldn't be a big deal. "Yes, there sure is. I'll do you one better. The body is Joshua Newkirk."

"The convicted rapist?" She let out a curse. "And he was killed in Miss Daniels's backyard?"

Tanner filled in his boss on all the details, including the lack of blood on scene.

"Tanner, I need you to be straight with me," the sheriff said after he'd finished. "It's no secret you're involved with Bree. Do I need to pull you off this case? I'm worried you can't stay neutral."

"The guy is dead. I'm not sure my neutrality makes any difference."

"You still have a killer to find, and it's no secret you weren't a fan of Newkirk's."

Tanner swallowed a curse. "I hope nobody was a fan of Newkirk's. Just because I'm not sad he's dead doesn't mean I won't bring down his killer."

Sheriff Duggan was quiet for a moment. One of the things Tanner appreciated the most about the woman he'd worked for for over ten years was that she thought things through before she spoke.

But when she did speak this time, it wasn't something he wanted to hear.

"I'm going to send Richard Whitaker out there. And before you start arguing with me, because I know you will, this is not a punishment or because I don't trust you. He's fresh eyes, and he doesn't have a history with either Bree or Newkirk."

Tanner knew this was what was best, but it still rankled. Not to mention nobody got along well with Richard Whitaker. The guy was a grade-A jerk.

"You know I don't like it, but I'm not going to fight you on it."

"Good. Because someone has been murdered. And whether we liked the dead guy or not, our job is to find out who did it."

Chapter Six

Richard Whitaker, Tanner's counterpart in the northern part of Grand County, showed up an hour later. Tanner and Ronnie met him out front as he pulled up.

"Whitaker." They both shook the man's hand.

"Dempsey. Kitchens." Richard nodded at them before tilting his head toward the crime scene in the back. "Sheriff said you finally had a little bit of excitement out here."

Tanner caught Ronnie's eyes roll in his peripheral. He couldn't blame the man. Everybody tended to want to roll their eyes around Richard Whitaker. The guy had moved here from Dallas six or seven years ago because his wife was from this area and wanted to return. Ironically, when they'd divorced eighteen months back, Richard had been the one who'd stayed and his wife had been the one who moved away.

Whitaker was a good cop. He had gotten quite a bit of experience in his years with the Dallas PD—a fact he never let anyone forget. But his disdain for small-town life and police work was pretty evident. Sometimes it was hard to understand why he stayed.

"Yeah. Victim's name is Joshua Newkirk. He was a convicted felon—a rapist." They walked toward the crime scene. Owen and his colleague were now searching for any blood traces that might show where Newkirk came from if he stumbled here on his own.

"Based on body temps," Ronnie continued, "looks like he's been dead a little over six hours. Body was called in a little over two hours ago."

"But Miss Daniels didn't call 911. Is that correct?" Whitaker looked pointedly at Tanner.

Tanner crossed his arms over his chest. "Yeah, that's right. She called me. She knows me. It's not a huge stretch."

"Maybe. But when I was on the Dallas force, a lot of times we would find the person who called in a crime had something to do with it. Seems like they thought it made them look more innocent."

Tanner stiffened. "Well, you're not in Dallas, and Bree didn't have anything to do with this."

Whitaker tilted his head to the side. "And that right there is the exact reason why the sheriff sent me out here. You're not neutral, Dempsey."

Tanner's teeth ground together. He stopped walking. "Just because I'm not going off chasing wild rabbits doesn't mean I'm not capable of finding out who did this to Newkirk."

Ronnie stopped next to him. "I'm not involved with Bree, so, by your definition, I'm much more neutral, and I concur with Tanner. I don't think she has the physical prowess to get the drop on someone Newkirk's size. Plus, I definitely don't think she's stupid enough to drop a body in her own backyard. The woman has an IQ of 832."

Whitaker looked like he was going to argue the point further, but finally he just nodded. "Fine. We won't concentrate on Miss Daniels at the moment. But if evidence suggests she had a part in this, I can damn well promise you I'm going to bring her in. Just because Risk Peak is a small town and everyone knows everyone else doesn't mean we're going to ignore facts and proper procedure."

Tanner could feel Ronnie rolling his eyes again. "Yeah, we get it," Tanner said. "Facts and solid procedure are the same regardless of whether you're in a big city or small town. But Bree didn't do this."

Whitaker gave another hard nod and walked the rest of the way to the body.

Tanner stayed behind and turned to Ronnie. "Can you finish up here with him? I'm going to take Bree out to the ranch so she can get some rest. I'll be back in this afternoon."

Ronnie slapped him on the shoulder. "Absolutely. I wish this hadn't happened in her backyard. Literally. She's been through enough."

Tanner scrubbed a hand over his face. "I know."

"Go take care of her."

The one good thing about Whitaker being here was that it allowed Tanner to leave with complete peace of mind, ironically, because of the man's big-city police force expertise. Whatever inexperience Ronnie may have working with a murder, Whitaker made up for. And the sheriff was right: two sets of eyes were always better than one.

But Whitaker was still a jerk.

Tanner walked through the back door of Bree's apartment and found her sitting at the kitchen table, hands wrapped around a mug. Exhaustion seemed to drip from her features. She looked more like she had when he first met her months ago—tired, haunted.

He hated it.

"Hey," he whispered. "You doing okay?"

Those green eyes that had enthralled him from the very first time he'd seen her looked up at him now.

"I'm okay. Just tired."

"Why don't you pack a bag? You can't stay here. I want to take you to the ranch."

Those eyes lit up a little. "Really?"

"Is that okay?"

She nodded with more energy. "Let me get my stuff."

A few minutes later, they were headed out to Tanner's SUV. "I'll just bring you in to work later. Is that okay? Then you can get your car. I know the drive will be a hassle, but I don't want you staying in town on your own."

"That's fine."

He opened the door for her, then went around and got in himself, starting the vehicle and pulling away.

He kept glancing over at her as he drove, waiting for some sort of outburst from her. But she actually looked a little happy.

"Why do you keep looking at me like that?" she asked when they were about ten minutes outside town.

"Occupational hazard, I guess. Just want to make sure you're all right. I wouldn't blame you if you were upset. Hell, I convinced you to move to Risk Peak because it was supposed to be a *safe place*. And now this happens."

She actually smiled at him. "I was most concerned the dead person was someone we knew. When you told me it wasn't, that was a huge relief. Plus, now I get to stay at the ranch. I'll get to see Star every day rather than having to wait five more weeks."

He couldn't help but smile back at her. That was Bree, wasn't it? She never quite reacted the way people would expect someone to.

It was one of the many reasons he was falling in love with her.

But then the smile fell off her face. "That's wrong, isn't it? How I'm feeling. I should be upset that someone is dead."

"Believe me, you not being hysterical is helpful in this situation."

She turned to look out the window and was silent for a long while. "But it's not normal. Once I found out it wasn't anyone we knew, I didn't really care that there was a dead body in my backyard. It was more stressful that there were so many people at the house than anything else. And it can't be normal that I care more about getting to the ranch and seeing a dog."

He grabbed her hands she was twisting in her lap. "Bree—"

She turned to him, face distraught. "I don't have correct emotions, Tanner. I'm broken."

He flipped on his hazard lights and pulled the SUV over to the side of the road, then turned to her, cupping her cheeks with both hands.

"I don't ever want to hear you say that again. Your emotions are just fine. Just because you're not hysterical doesn't mean you're broken. Never feel bad for how your brilliant mind fortifies you so you can survive."

"But—"

"No buts." He reached between them and kissed her briefly. "You survived what would've broken most people. And you're amazing just the way you are."

He wasn't sure if she believed him, but he meant every word. He waited until she finally nodded before releasing her and pulling back on the road again.

It wasn't long before they were arriving at the ranch. He grabbed her overnight bag, and they walked inside.

"We both need to get a few hours' sleep," he said. "I'll take the couch and you can have the bed."

She walked toward the bedroom but turned at the door. "Come with me. Just to sleep together like before." Those big green eyes studied him as she reached her hand out toward him.

There was nothing he wanted more than to curl up with her in his bed. But with his anger and frustration so close to the surface, he couldn't discount the fact that he might wake up swinging. The thought of Bree being the recipient of his night terrors made him break out into a cold sweat.

"Never mind," she said quickly, misreading his hesitation, hand falling back to her side. "You don't have to."

Damn it, he'd rather never sleep again than see that wounded look in her eyes from something he'd done.

He stepped toward her. "I want to. Trust me, there's nothing I want more. But...I just don't want to take a chance on waking you up if I get called back in to Risk Peak early." That was at least a partial truth.

The haunted look fell away from her eyes, and a shy smile broke on her face. "I don't mind. I'll take a shorter amount of sleep if it means I get to sleep next to you."

He would have given her anything in the world to keep that sweet smile on her face. He took her hand, and they walked into the bedroom together.

They took turns changing into sleep clothes in the bathroom, then got into the bed together. The act was so innocent and yet so intimate.

Tanner rolled over onto his side and pulled Bree's

back against his front. He breathed in the sweet scent of her hair as her head rested in the crook of his elbow. His other arm wrapped loosely around her waist.

She was out within minutes, her smaller body relaxing against him, trusting him to shelter and protect her while she slept. Tanner wouldn't betray that trust, even if that meant protecting her against himself.

Besides, sleeping was overrated when he could be awake and feel every curve that had been haunting his dreams for months pressed against him.

Definitely worth it.

Chapter Seven

"Coffee?"

The fact that Ronnie was already at Tanner's desk with a cup of the steaming brew right under his nose before Tanner even realized he was in the room was testament to Tanner's exhaustion.

It had been a hell of a week. He'd spent all day every day working the Newkirk murder case. Running into dead end after dead end.

And then night after night near Bree, loving being around her but trying not to let her get too close. It was a fine line he was walking with her. They needed to have a long conversation about his PTSD as soon as this case was done.

Because there was no way he was going to be able to keep his hands off her for much longer.

Tanner took the cup from Ronnie and nearly scalded himself as he swallowed a gulp. "I was looking over the suspect list again, hoping something might jump out at me this time."

Ronnie grabbed the tennis ball that rested on

Tanner's desk and began bouncing it. Bounce the ball as they bounced around ideas. They'd been doing it for as long as they'd been working in this building together. "Maybe Whitaker will have some insight after talking to Newkirk's family again."

Tanner nodded. At least the other cop was out of their hair. He'd finally left yesterday after being in Risk Peak for three days.

The few details they had about the murder were set out in the case file on Tanner's desk. Joshua Newkirk had been stabbed in the back six times. He'd definitely been wrapped and transported into Bree's yard. The crime lab team had not found any traces of blood anywhere around the body. So there was no way he could've stumbled into her yard of his own accord.

Whitaker had not taken Tanner's insistence that Bree was innocent at face value. Only after thoroughly investigating any possible ties between her and Newkirk and coming up empty had Whitaker deemed her cleared. He'd even brought her in for questioning, which Tanner chalked up to just wanting to piss him off.

He set down his coffee cup and held up his hand so Ronnie could toss him the ball. "Why Bree's place? That's the only thing about this that doesn't sit right with me. Why dump the body in Bree's yard?"

Ronnie nodded. "It's not like there's any shortage of people who might want to kill Newkirk. Guy has enemies all over the state. But nothing to do with her."

Tanner bounced the ball back to him. "And he had no real ties to Risk Peak. I was part of the group who arrested him, but I was helping to work the case up north. I didn't even have a major role in any of it."

Ronnie flipped the ball back and forth between his hands. "Yeah, I don't get it, either. I'm hoping Whitaker comes up with something after today."

Tanner sighed. "As long as it doesn't mean he has to come spend three more days here."

"Maybe we could start a pool to guess how many times in a day Whitaker will say the words *Dallas* or *big city*." Ronnie tossed the ball back to him.

He chuckled. "I'd be down for a piece of that action."

"Is Bree doing okay? I can't blame her for not wanting to move back into her apartment. Hell, Cindy would make us move to an entirely new place altogether if a body showed up in our yard."

"Bree's doing good. I don't think she'll have any problem moving back into her apartment. I just want to give her however much time she needs." Tanner set the ball back on his desk.

He'd brought up the topic of moving back into Risk Peak very casually with her yesterday. He didn't want her to feel like he was forcing her away from the ranch.

It would probably be best for her to move back to town. That way she wouldn't have to drive so far to get to work every day, and he could get a good night's sleep in his own bed without having to worry about hurting her.

But hell if he wanted that. He liked having her on the ranch. Definitely because he knew she was safe, but also because he liked having her around. For meals. For coffee in the morning out on the porch. For watching her play with that damned puppy.

But he couldn't go on the way he'd been going. He was way past burning the candle at both ends— his life was more of a roaring bonfire at both ends. He wasn't getting the sleep he needed, and knowing that Bree was wondering about the distance he kept between them ate at him.

Definitely time for a talk about what had happened to him on that undercover op three years ago. How it had affected and changed him. How PTSD might be something he had to live with for the rest of his life.

But it was something he hated to talk about. Just ask Dr. Michalski. He'd been trying to drag details out of Tanner for three years.

Tanner also didn't want to talk about it with her since Bree had known such pain in her own young life. He didn't want to add to her burden by asking her to help carry his trauma also.

But not talking wasn't going to make it go away. Bree was part of his life now. The biggest and most important part. If he couldn't get his PTSD under control, then it was something that he had to share with her so she understood what was going on.

But damn it, he wished he could be someone who just came to her with no baggage. She deserved that. Deserved someone who could help her carry her own.

"Until we hear from Whitaker, I'm just going to put the Newkirk case on the back burner."

Tanner looked up at Ronnie. "Yeah. Nothing we can do."

"Also, high on the fun scale...we've promised Mr. Dunwoody that we would stake out his auto shop over the next week and try to discover who's vandalizing him. So I'm going to be out there for the graveyard shift tonight."

Dunwoody's auto repair shop was on the southeast edge of the county, in the middle of nowhere. Much to Mr. Dunwoody's chagrin, someone kept breaking into his shop and painting rainbows everywhere. Mr. Dunwoody threatened to wait for it to happen again with his shotgun ready, but Tanner had talked him into letting them try to catch the vandals first. Especially since it was probably teenagers from the nearby high school.

"Great. I guess I'm lucky and get tomorrow night's shift, then."

Ronnie rolled his eyes. "Maybe we'll get lucky and I'll catch them tonight. Pacify Mr. Dunwoody."

Ronnie gave a little salute and walked out of the office. It was time for Tanner to go also. All the stuff involving Newkirk, Mr. Dunwoody or any of Risk Peak's other problems would have to wait. Even the hard talk he needed to have with Bree would have to wait.

Tonight he was leaving this behind. Taking Bree to possibly his favorite place on earth. It was exactly what he needed, and he was looking forward to it. Tonight would be the opposite of what the rest of his week had been. It would be fun, relaxed, easy.

TONIGHT WAS GOING to be a total disaster.

Bree sat in the living room of Tanner's house, smoothing her palms along her skirt. It was a cute skirt, a flowy navy blue with little white flowers. It came down to just above her knees and looked great with the matching white blouse. Tanner had loved it when she'd worn it for a date a couple of weeks ago, but now she just wanted to rip it off and throw it away.

Of course, that probably had less to do with the outfit and more to do with the fact that Tanner was taking her to have dinner with his family. How could this go any way but poorly?

Before she could think of an excuse not to go, Tanner pulled up.

The way his breath whistled out between his teeth and he stared at her made her feel better. But only for a moment. "You look absolutely edible."

Whatever argument she was about to make to try to get out of dinner disappeared when he stalked toward her. That was the only word for it: *stalked*. Like he was a predator and she was his prey.

And he had every intention of eating her up.

It should scare her, make her wary, but all it did was light up the most feminine parts of her.

He was on her in just a second, one strong arm wrapping around her hips and spinning her until she was pressed up against the living room wall. He pressed up against her, and all thoughts fled from her head when he claimed her lips.

His mouth was demanding as he tilted his head, moving hers with it, giving him the angle he wanted. She moaned as his tongue traced the seam of her lips, and she opened for him. The kiss deepened, his tongue sliding over hers, tasting her. Claiming her.

When his hand fisted her skirt, sliding it up, and she felt his fingers skim along the outside of her thigh, she pressed herself closer. Trying to concentrate on the kiss was impossible with the lines his fingers were trailing up and down her hip and thigh.

"Damn it." He was breathing as hard as she was as he pulled away a few minutes later, his forehead dropping against hers. "We've got to stop this or we're going to be late and my mother will kill me. I've got to change and shave. My five o'clock shadow is a little out of control."

She reached up and touched his cheek. "I like your scruff. It's sexy." It made him look a little dangerous.

His hand covered hers on his cheek. "We met because of this scruff, you know. I caught you shoplifting in the drugstore because Mr. Vanover keeps my special razor refills in the back aisle. If he didn't, I probably never would've been back there or seen you."

She ran her fingernails along the short whiskers. "I'm glad you caught me," she whispered. "It's the best thing that ever happened to me."

Heat seemed to pool in his soft brown eyes. The hand that wasn't covering hers on his cheek wrapped around her waist, anchoring her against him.

She could feel the hardness of him pressed up against her. For just a second she was tempted to throw caution to the wind and see if she could seduce him into staying. But she quickly pushed the thought aside. She didn't want their first time to be because she had emotionally manipulated him in order to get out of a dinner.

Not to mention she didn't know how to seduce a man anyway.

He groaned and pulled back. "You're going to be the death of me."

"Is that a good thing or bad thing?"

"The very best of things. Now, you wait right here five minutes. It's time for the most important people in my life to get to know each other better."

Chapter Eight

Bree wanted to run; she really did. She wanted to run when Tanner made it back to the living room four and a half minutes later looking mouthwatering himself in jeans and a button-down shirt.

She definitely wanted to run when they pulled up to his mother's house thirty minutes after that.

Bree had met all of Tanner's family before. Noah at the ranch, of course. Mrs. Dempsey and Tanner's sister, Cassandra, came to town sometimes and to the Sunrise. It was impossible not to have met them in a town the size of Risk Peak. But this was the first time she was facing them as Tanner's girlfriend.

Grasping the box filled with Mrs. Andrews's lemon pie from the Sunrise Diner, she walked stiffly with him toward the door.

He slid an arm around her shoulders and pulled her close, kissing her temple. "You're going to do great. They're going to love you."

Bree was not nearly as sure about either of those things. This situation was pretty much her worst nightmare—a small group where she was expected to interact and banter wittily.

So basically to act like a normal person with normal personal interaction skills.

Yeah, this was not going to go well.

Dinner actually went by without her making any terrible faux pas. Between Tanner and Cassandra's constant bickering, with Noah and Cassandra's husband, Graham, occasionally chiming in, there wasn't much conversation that was expected from Bree. Every once in a while, Mrs. Dempsey would try to bring her brood under control, but it was easy to see that the fighting was in good fun. Graham and Cassandra's three kids, all between the ages of eight and twelve, ate as fast as they could then begged to be excused to go back out to the fishing pond. Cassandra agreed, sending them with the cookies she'd baked.

As soon as they were gone, she turned back to the adults at the table. "I'm no idiot. I made cookies for the kids so there's more pie for us."

"Damn it, I thought I was the smartest one in this family," Tanner muttered.

When everyone got up and started carrying their dishes into the kitchen, Bree grabbed hers and followed suit.

"How are you enjoying living on the ranch?" Mrs. Dempsey asked. "It's always been too isolated for my tastes. Is it the same for you? It must be much different than Kansas City."

Bree's life in Kansas City had been pretty isolated also. She'd been surrounded by people, but still alone.

"No, I actually like the isolation. Sometimes a lot of people can be a little too much for me."

"Amen to that," Noah muttered. "Give me horses over people any day."

Tanner smiled and kissed her on the top of the head as he passed by with some dishes.

"Yeah, but what's it like living with my idiot brother?" Cassandra elbowed Tanner as she walked into the kitchen.

Bree wasn't sure what to say. They weren't really living together. Would Mrs. Dempsey think Bree was some sort of freeloader? "I'm only living there because of the crime scene at my house and the puppy."

Cassandra grinned as she and Tanner sat back down. "Not if Tanner has anything to say about it."

Bree could feel heat rising in her cheeks. She had no idea what she was supposed to say to that. "Um…"

"Ow!" Cassandra glared at Tanner. "Mom, Tanner just pinched me under the table."

Mrs. Dempsey turned to them. "You two behave. Bree, why don't we leave the infants alone and go cut the pie."

They could hear Cassandra and the boys yelling and laughing as they left.

"Are they really arguing?" Bree asked.

Mrs. Dempsey rolled her eyes. "Cassandra is

the baby. She likes to stir up trouble when both her brothers are here. Do you have siblings?"

"No, it was just me." She'd barely even had a mom growing up.

Mrs. Dempsey began cutting the pie. "My son doesn't bring someone home for a family dinner lightly. He's quite smitten with you."

"I...I..." Some days Bree wasn't sure he was. For the past days, even though she'd lived in the same house as him, he'd seemed to keep himself so distant. Not like he resented having her there, but like she was a guest who he liked but wanted to keep a respectful distance from.

But then today...that kiss against the wall. There had been nothing like that all the other days. Nothing like that, ever. Where he'd kissed her like he was about to lose control.

And she'd loved it. She could still feel the ghost of his fingers on her outer thigh.

But was Tanner *smitten* with her, like his mother suggested? "I don't know. Sometimes, I just don't know."

Mrs. Dempsey looked up from the pie and studied Bree. "Tanner has his own demons—pretty significant ones—and his own way of handling them."

"He does?" He was so laid-back and friendly. He seemed so likable and approachable. It had never really occurred to her that he might have demons like her.

"He doesn't talk to you about stuff?"

Bree shook her head. "Some. But no, not stuff like that."

Mrs. Dempsey's tone hadn't been judgmental in any way, but the words themselves made Bree recognize once again that maybe she wasn't meeting Tanner's needs. Maybe that was why they still hadn't slept together.

Mrs. Dempsey reached over and squeezed Bree's arm. "He's protective of you. I can't blame him—you've got something special that makes him want to take care of you. To fight all your battles for you. Tanner's dad felt that way about me."

Mrs. Dempsey didn't look like someone who needed protecting. She looked like she could fight her own battles.

"Of course, I had to set Clifford straight pretty early on in our relationship. Because it was never going to be enough for me—or for him—to let him wrap me in cotton wool. It is enough for some women and some relationships, but it wasn't what either Clifford or I needed. Is it what you need, Bree?"

Bree's answer was immediate. "No. I've been taking care of myself for a long time. Probably longer than I should've. I'm strong."

Mrs. Dempsey smiled at her. "I believe that. You've definitely got a core of steel. You're probably going to need to convince Tanner that you're strong enough to be what he needs, though."

What did Tanner need? Bree wasn't sure. She

might've asked Mrs. Dempsey if shouting hadn't started from the dining room.

"We want pie! We want pie!"

Mrs. Dempsey sighed and grinned. "Looks like the natives are getting restless. Shall we?"

All of the Dempsey siblings began eyeing the pie in Mrs. Dempsey's hand as soon as she walked in the room.

"Hey, Mom," Tanner said, innocence all but dripping from his voice. "Is there any pie left in the box, you know, for after we're done? Asking for a friend."

Mrs. Dempsey's eyes narrowed. "If I say yes, are you going to forget every manner I ever taught you?"

"No, ma'am," all three Dempsey siblings and Graham responded at the same time.

She just rolled her eyes. "Then yes, there's one piece left."

Bree's jaw dropped as Tanner, Noah and Graham accepted their pie and began scarfing it down. She glanced over at Cassandra, but she was eating hers at a more humanlike rate. She shrugged. "I gave up my horse in this race when I got married. I might've been able to outeat one of my brothers, but there was no way to beat them and Graham. Although sometimes if I promise hubby here sexual favors he'll give me some of the pie if he wins." She wagged her eyebrows. Graham gave her a thumbs-up with one hand and kept piling in pie with the other.

Bree just smiled, watching the eating with wonder. "Tanner tried to explain the whole pie thing to me once. But really you have to see it in person to truly understand."

As soon as the men finished their pie—within seconds of each other—they made comically polite excuses before rushing toward the kitchen. This entire process was obviously a time-honored tradition.

Cassandra and Mrs. Dempsey just shook their heads, both eating their pie at a much more leisurely pace.

"So," Cassandra said. "How are you liking waiting tables at the Sunrise Diner?"

"Cass," Mrs. Dempsey said quietly.

Cassandra shrugged. "No harm in me talking to her about it."

Bree didn't mind talking about her job. Did Mrs. Dempsey think she was sensitive about it?

"I like it. Dan and Cheryl have always been very supportive."

"Do you miss working with computers?" Cassandra asked.

Bree stared down at her pie. Tanner probably hadn't told his family very much about her past. This conversation had turned stressful amazingly quickly. What was the most appropriate way to answer Cassandra's question?

She brought a piece of pie to her mouth, more to buy herself time than anything else. How did she feel about computers? Pinpointing it wasn't easy.

"It's complicated," she finally said.

"How so?" Cassandra asked.

"Cass…" Mrs. Dempsey said again.

"I'm not doing any harm, Mom. Just trying to understand."

Bree was somehow causing tension between Cassandra and her mother. She didn't want that. "I'm good with computers, but because of some of the stuff that happened when I was a kid, they sometimes hold triggers for me."

Cassandra nodded, her eyes narrowing. "Do you think you'll ever work with them again?"

Bree shifted in her chair. She wasn't sure why Cassandra was asking her that. Were they worried she might do something illegal and drag Tanner down with her? They had to know that she had ties to the Organization. Did they think she was involved with the evil stuff they'd done?

Before Bree could think of what to say, Cassandra continued. "I'm a hairdresser by trade. I have my cosmetology license."

Bree blinked at the change in subject. "Oh. I've never seen you working in town."

"I don't, at least not very often anymore. I stay home with the kids now. But I'm starting a part-time project. A mission, sort of."

The guys came back in from the kitchen, all three of them grinning but looking a little disheveled. "We shared."

"Is my kitchen still in one piece?" Mrs. Dempsey raised one brow.

"Yes, ma'am," all three said dutifully.

"I was just telling Bree about the shelter," Cassandra said. "I had an idea and wanted to get her opinion."

Tanner sat in the chair next to Bree and put his arm along the back, playing with the hair at her nape. Everyone in his family noticed the possessive touch, but none of them seemed upset about it. That was good, right? It meant they liked her?

"What did you want Bree's opinion about?" Tanner asked.

Cassandra ignored his question and looked at Bree. "I'm part of a privately funded group in Grand County that is starting a women's shelter. We are just far enough outside Denver to help women from there trying to get out of domestic violence situations."

Bree nodded, still not quite understanding what opinion Cassandra wanted from her, but if it was enthusiasm for this venture, Bree could definitely give that. "That sounds amazing."

"A friend of ours in Colorado Springs—" Cassandra gestured between herself and Tanner "—Keira Weber, started one there. Not only is it a safe place for women to stay, she teaches them a trade, how to cut and style hair."

Bree nodded. That was a great idea, too. Logical. Practical. It not only helped the women get back on their feet, it provided them a means to provide for themselves long-term. "It sounds like a very noble venture, and a smart way of going about it."

Cassandra smiled. "I wanted to get your opinion

about offering some basic computer classes to these women. Providing them skills that would be most useful in an office workplace."

That was also a good idea. Bree was just about to say so when Cassandra continued. "And I wanted to see if you'd be interested in teaching the classes."

Bree jerked ramrod straight and stared at her for a moment before a slightly hysterical laugh fell from her lips.

That was a terrible idea. She would be a horrible teacher. Standing up in front of a group of people, trying to explain things? Definitely not a good plan.

She glanced down at her hands. But...these would be women who needed help. People who were like her, or how she'd been when she first wandered into Risk Peak. Alone, desperate, broke. Their situation wouldn't be exactly the same, of course, but still... Similar.

Could she do it? Could she figure out a way to help these women the way people in Risk Peak had helped her?

A clanging of a plate against another brought her attention back to the table. Cassandra had stood up and was stacking the remaining pie plates on the table.

"Cass," Tanner said. "You should've talked to me about this first."

Cassandra turned to Bree. "Sorry you think the idea of women learning computer skills is laughable. I thought maybe you could see the bigger picture."

"No, that's not what I meant." Bree gave a panicked look at Tanner before turning back to Cassandra. "I *do* think it's a good idea."

"Cass, you don't have all the facts here," Tanner said. His phone buzzed at his waist, and he grabbed it and looked down at it. "Damn it. This is the station. Gotta take it."

Tanner walked out of the room, leaving Bree with his family.

"Cassandra, I..."

"You know what? Don't worry about it." Cassandra took the plates and walked into the kitchen. Graham followed her in with an apologetic shrug.

"Just ignore her," Noah said. "That's what we do."

Mrs. Dempsey reached over and patted Bree's arm. "Don't worry about it, honey. Cassandra is very passionate and her heart is in the right place, but she doesn't always think everything through."

"I wasn't trying to say the *idea* was bad, just the idea of me teaching it may not be so great."

The older woman smiled. "We'll talk to her and explain. Nobody wants you to do anything you're uncomfortable with."

Bree almost laughed again but caught herself. If they knew she was uncomfortable just having a regular conversation like this, they'd probably think she was an idiot.

But before Cassandra came back in and Bree could try to explain her communication faux pas, Tanner entered the room.

"Sorry, Mom. I'm going to have to cut things short. Ronnie has some sort of food poisoning, and we promised Mr. Dunwoody we'd scope out his shop tonight. Try to figure out who is vandalizing it."

Bree all but jumped out of her chair. Leaving seemed like a great option, since she'd already ruined the evening.

Tanner hugged his family, and Cassandra caught Bree just before they went out the door.

"Listen, I hate it when my husband is all logical and stuff, but he pointed out that I blindsided you. And he's right. That wasn't fair."

Bree nodded rapidly. "I do think it's an excellent idea. I just don't think I'm a good teacher. You could do much better."

Cassandra smiled. "Actually, I don't think we could do better. Tanner says you're a genius with a computer. And he doesn't throw that word around lightly."

Bree just shrugged.

Cassandra grabbed her hand and gave it a squeeze. "Just think about it. What you know and could teach these women could make a huge difference in their lives. Not only because of what you would teach them, but because you understand some of what they're going through. You're right—a number of people could teach them computer skills. But it's *you* who could really make a difference."

Chapter Nine

Tanner woke up the next morning—he glanced over at the clock, nope, the next *afternoon*—feeling better after a few solid hours of sleep.

He'd stayed outside Dunwoody's shop until just after 4:00 a.m. There had been absolutely nothing going on near there, and despite multiple cups of coffee, Tanner had been falling asleep in his vehicle. Finally, he'd just decided to give up and head home. Evidently the wicked rainbow painters weren't out that night.

He'd hoped to catch Bree here, but she'd already gone to work, which was probably for the best. After that kiss yesterday afternoon, Tanner didn't know if he could lie in the same bed with her again and not do anything about it.

He wasn't a man given to fancifulness, but the skin of her thigh had been so soft he could damn near write poetry about it.

Seeing her around his family hadn't cooled his ardor, either. He liked watching her with them, seeing how she fit in, even when she was uncomfortable and unsure of herself thanks to Cassandra. His sister could be a lot for anyone to handle, and he wanted to wring her neck for dropping the computer-teaching bomb on Bree.

Bree might have gotten upset initially, but they'd spent the entire ride home talking about what computer skills would most help the women at the shelter. Bree had a basic syllabus all but planned out by the time they'd gotten back to the ranch. It was easy for him to see that, despite her hesitation, she was going to teach the class. Now he just needed to wait for her to realize it, too.

Watching her face her fears and step up to help others was pretty damn amazing. *Bree* was pretty damn amazing.

So yeah, it was probably better she hadn't been there this morning, or else he definitely wouldn't have been keeping his hands off her.

Tanner made himself a sandwich for lunch, washing it down with a big mug of coffee. He was outside checking on Corfu and the pups when Noah came riding up on one of his horses. He got off and quickly put the horse in the corral.

"You expecting company?" Noah asked.

"No." Most people knew better than to come out here without being invited or calling first. Noah was not a people person.

"Looks like one of the Grand County sheriff's vehicles."

Tanner grabbed his phone out of his pocket to see

if he'd missed any calls. Nothing. "I have no idea. They haven't tried to contact me."

Noah nodded then faded back into the wooded area surrounding their property, making himself unnoticeable. But Tanner had no doubt he'd be out in a second if he was needed.

Less than a minute later, the vehicle arrived outside Tanner's door. Noah had been right—it was a Grand County SUV. But it wasn't any of Tanner's regular colleagues who was driving; it was Richard Whitaker.

"Dempsey," he said as he got out of the vehicle.

Tanner raised an eyebrow. "You lost, Whitaker? Dallas is about eight hundred miles south of here."

The other man pointed to Tanner's cup of coffee. "Just now waking up?"

"As a matter of fact, yes. The stakeout I was on last night didn't amount to anything, so I left. I called in that I was going home."

Whitaker crossed his arms over his beefy chest. "I know."

For the first time Tanner was a little more worried than confused about Whitaker's appearance at his home. "Why are you here?"

"Sheriff wants to see you in her office."

"Why? Has there been a break in the Newkirk case?"

Whitaker shrugged. "Possibly. I'll let the sheriff talk to you about that. Did you go anywhere else besides your high-crime stakeout?"

Tanner ignored the small-town barb. "No. I'd already put in a full day then came back to work someone else's shift."

"You must've been tired. Why'd you come all the way out here rather than your place in Risk Peak?"

Tanner wasn't going to discuss his relationship with Bree and that he'd wanted to see her. It was none of Whitaker's business. "Why are you asking so many questions? Why are you here at all? The sheriff could've just called me herself and asked me to come in."

Whitaker shrugged. "I'll let the sheriff answer that, too. I'm just here to make sure you get to her with no problems."

That was definitely not a good sign.

Tanner gave a curt nod. "I'll follow you in."

Less than an hour later, he was sitting across from Sheriff Duggan in her office. She'd invited Whitaker in also and then closed the door.

"I'll cut straight to the chase, Tanner." She walked back and took a seat in the office chair behind her desk. The same chair that had once been Tanner's father's when he'd been sheriff. "Peter Anders is dead."

A low curse fell from Tanner's mouth, although he could admit he wasn't terribly surprised. Anders had been in and out of prison for the entire eight years Tanner had known him. Tanner had been the one to arrest him more than once.

He scrubbed a hand over his face. "When? How?"

Sheriff Duggan looked over at Whitaker before bringing her eyes back to Tanner. "Roughly nine hours ago. The body was found about an hour later. He was stabbed multiple times in the back."

"Like Newkirk," Tanner said.

Whitaker crossed his arms over his chest. "Yeah, exactly like Newkirk."

Tanner shifted to look at him. "I hope you're not considering Bree as a suspect again." Because Tanner damn well wasn't going to stand for it.

Whitaker's eyes narrowed. "No, *Bree* isn't our suspect."

The implication was clear, but Tanner turned back to the sheriff, wanting to make sure he understood. "What exactly is Dallas PD implying over here?"

Before she could respond, Whitaker spoke again. "Is there anybody who can verify your whereabouts last night?"

"I was on a stakeout at Dunwoody's auto shop in the southeast corner of the county. They've had some vandals. We think it's high school kids and wanted to put a stop to it before Dunwoody decided to take matters into his own hands with buckshot."

"Anyone see you out there?" Whitaker demanded.

"No. There was nothing happening, so I went home." Tanner looked over at the sheriff. "I called everything in. It's all logged."

Whitaker shifted his weight in the chair, looking over at Tanner, eyes narrowed. "You went all the way back to your ranch when you could've just gone to your place in town."

Damn it, Tanner still wasn't going to drag Bree's name into this. Especially since he hadn't actually seen her this morning and she couldn't provide an alibi anyway. "Yes. I have a place in town, but the ranch is my home. Everybody knows that."

"It's also a lot more isolated," Whitaker quipped. "You're quite a bit less likely to be seen there. If, say, you needed to wash up or something."

Tanner jerked out of his chair, nearly knocking it over in his fury. "What exactly are you saying?"

"Hey, I'm just—"

"Enough, Whitaker," the sheriff cut in.

Tanner ran a hand through his hair, getting himself under control, but he was too agitated to sit back down. "Fine. I get that someone else whose arrest I was involved in is dead, and that sucks. But to jump straight into accusing me of washing blood off my hands? What the hell?"

The sheriff held out one hand toward him. "You're right, Tanner. And I don't believe you had anything to do with Anders's death."

"Her belief is the only reason you're not in cuffs in an interview room rather than in an office," Whitaker muttered.

Sheriff Duggan slammed her palm down on her desk then pointed at Whitaker. "You watch it. The Dempsey reputation is multigenerational and stellar. So you can either present the facts with respect and let your colleague provide his refutation or you can get the hell out of my office."

Whitaker shrank a little in his chair. "Yes, ma'am."

And somehow, even though it should make him feel better, that exchange made Tanner even more concerned.

"Sit down, Tanner," she said. "Tell us about your relationship with Peter Anders."

He rubbed a hand down his face as he sat. "I first arrested him eight years ago. He's been in and out of prison since then. Tends toward violent crimes. Assault. Assault and battery. Has—*had*—a pretty nasty temper."

"And like Newkirk, you also reported to Anders's parole board that you thought he shouldn't be let out." Whitaker's more reasonable tone didn't reassure him.

He met the sheriff's eye. "Look, I'll be honest—I do that with a lot of people. I get these requests for my opinion from review boards, and I give it honestly. Most of the time I do think the criminals should serve closer to their full sentence. A lot of times it feels like we're fighting a losing battle if the prison system just dumps them back on the streets too soon. But…"

"But what?" she asked.

Tanner sat forward and leaned his arms on his knees. "Peter got out almost a year ago after his latest charge—a bar brawl where he put a guy in a coma. But this time Peter seemed different. He'd found religion or something. I don't know. I really thought he was trying to change."

"So you've been in contact with him?" Sheriff Duggan asked.

Tanner shrugged one shoulder. "Some. Trying to help him get a job and get away from the people and situations that always seem to land him back in prison."

"You ever been in Anders's car?" Whitaker asked.

Tanner nodded. "Yes, a couple of weeks ago. He wouldn't come inside the station to talk, so I went out to him."

Whitaker gave a tiny snort of disbelief. "Convenient."

Tanner turned to glare at the man. "If anything, that shows I wasn't trying to kill him."

Sheriff Duggan nodded. "I can see that. But here's the real problem. We found this." She tapped on an electronic tablet then spun it around so Tanner could see it. "This is a copy of all Anders's texts for the last few days. We need you to address one in particular, Tanner."

Tanner looked down at the one she was pointing to.

Peter: I can't get rid of this Dempsey cop. He's on my ass all the time.

Bugaboo2: Just tell him to go to hell.

Peter: Cop is scary. He's threatening me. Seriously. So I'm a no-go for this weekend. Sorry.

Tanner tensed. "That's not what it looks like. I knew some of his old friends were pressuring him back into the lifestyle he was trying to get out of. I told him to use me as an excuse to say no."

Whitaker raised an eyebrow. "Convenient that it's your word against someone who can't say anything further."

Tanner turned to the sheriff. With every passing minute, this was looking worse and worse for him. "Do I need a lawyer? I feel a little like I need a lawyer."

The sheriff shook her head. "You're not being formally charged. I already talked to Ryan Fletcher this morning. He has no interest in pursuing this case at this time. Says it's all circumstantial. And, like me, he doesn't think you had anything to do with it."

Tanner nodded.

Whitaker all but threw up his hands. "We've got Dempsey's fingerprints in the victim's car. A text from the vic claiming Dempsey was threatening him. And he's got no alibi. *Worse* than no alibi."

Tanner's eyebrows narrowed. "What the hell is worse than no alibi?"

He expected Sheriff Duggan to jump in, too, but she didn't. When he glanced over, her lips were tight.

"Worse than no alibi is that the place you were supposedly staking out was vandalized last night," Whitaker said. "Guess you missed it, if you were even there at all. Of course, *not* being there would've given you plenty of time to drive to get to Anders, even if he was across the county."

"Or I stayed at the Dunwoody shop like I said, and the vandals came in after I left around four in the morning."

Whitaker held both hands out in front of him and shrugged. "Just sayin'. Anybody else would already be in a holding cell."

"But we're not dealing with someone else," Sheriff Duggan interjected. "Tanner has no motive for killing either Newkirk or Anders."

"Except they were both violent criminals that kept getting put back on the streets," Whitaker said in a low, reasonable voice. That voice was so much more dangerous than his yelled threats. "Dempsey said it himself. Sometimes you feel like you're fighting a losing battle. Maybe he decided to do something about it."

Sheriff Duggan steepled her fingers in front of her lips. "Like I said, I don't think you did this. But until we get it sorted out, you're going to need to go on admin leave. I need your badge and your gun, Tanner."

He remained silent, not even glancing at Whitaker as he took both off his belt and slid them across the desk.

The sheriff took them and put them in a drawer. "I still need you to schedule a visit with Dr. Michalski. He told me you've missed the last couple of scheduled sessions."

Tanner gritted his teeth. "I was busy."

Whitaker gave a slight cough/laugh. Tanner wanted

to punch him in the face but refrained, knowing it wouldn't do anything but get him more admin leave. He stood.

"We'll be in touch soon, Tanner," the sheriff said. "Give us a chance to work on your behalf. Take this time to get caught up on your appointments with Dr. Michalski and any reports you're behind on. That way when the dust clears, you're able to hit the ground running. We're all on the same side."

Tanner gave a terse nod then walked out into the hallway, still wanting to punch someone.

Finding Dr. Michalski standing right there did not diminish that feeling.

"What are you, waiting for me to come out of the principal's office?"

"You missed our last two sessions." The psychiatrist's expression and tone were even. The way they always were.

But seriously, did the guy have his ear at the door?

Tanner stuffed his hands in his pockets, conspicuously aware of the lack of familiar weight his gun and badge usually placed on his waist. "Sorry, Doc. I had real police work to do. Thought that took priority over rehashing past events in my life that can't ever be changed."

"I understand police work, Tanner. And I would've thought nothing of it if you'd just rescheduled like you're required to do. The rules apply to you, too."

Tanner grimaced. Because damn it, the man— and his goddamned even tone—was right. But hell if he was going to admit that right now, when he'd just basically been told that while the sheriff didn't think he was guilty, she didn't think he was innocent enough to keep wearing the badge.

"Yeah, I'll get around to it."

Dr. Michalski just nodded. "Be careful. That sort of arrogance can get you killed in this line of work. We work together as a team or everything crumbles quickly."

Tanner took his hand out of his pocket and rubbed his eyes. The thing was, he totally agreed with the doctor. Mental health was important. Just as important as physical health. The country was figuring that out the hard way.

The work he'd done with Dr. Michalski had helped him come to grips with some of what had happened in that warehouse three years ago. Tanner didn't always enjoy the company of the other man, but he had to admit their sessions had been valuable.

"Fine," he mumbled, brushing past the doctor. He couldn't do it right now. He just needed to get out of here.

"Make an appointment," the doctor said in a just slightly louder but still even tone. "And keep it this time."

Chapter Ten

The man couldn't keep the smile from his face.

And why should he even try? There was something downright delightful about knowing Tanner Dempsey was on his way down.

There wasn't enough info against him to arrest Dempsey—*yet*. But the seeds of doubt had been planted in the minds that counted in the most delicious way possible.

How had it felt to Dempsey to be summoned from his own home to the sheriff's office, like the criminal that he was?

How did it feel to Mr. High and Mighty to know that people doubted him? To realize they were starting to see the crack in his veneer and would soon know him for what he really was: a fraud and a lying, judgmental bastard.

Oh, and a killer.

How did it feel when the pedestal he'd placed himself on started to show signs of rust and decay? Was he unable to sleep at night, knowing he was going to fall?

Did he worry when he realized the blood on his hands and deceit in his heart would become visible to everyone soon?

Including the woman who occupied Dempsey's every thought. He'd had the gall to move her in with him, even knowing what he was.

But no worries. She would see the facts soon, along with everyone else. No one would be able to ignore the truth any longer. She would watch as Dempsey was finally sentenced for his sins and spent the rest of his life rotting in jail.

She would be sad, but maybe the man could step up and comfort her. That would be a beautiful full circle.

So yes, the man's smile was huge. He had to keep his colleagues from seeing it and asking him what was going on.

Because he just might tell them.

Justice was finally about to be served.

Chapter Eleven

When Bree pulled up to the ranch, she found Tanner chopping wood. He'd chopped enough wood in the past three days to last all of Risk Peak through the winter.

Being on suspension obviously did not sit well with Captain Sexy Lips.

He'd explained that the sheriff didn't actually think Tanner had committed the two murders, so that was good. It was just a matter of staying out of the way while the other people in the department worked the case. But he definitely did not like being kept in the dark about what was going on with the investigation.

For the past three days, the fact that she had no idea how to help him had eaten at her. Just another glaring spotlight on her lack of interpersonal relationship skills. Usually it was *him* helping *her* figure out how to sort through feelings. But for the last three days, the shoe had been on the other foot.

Not a good fit.

Bree had tried her best to cheer him up or take his mind off his problems, but she didn't really know how. Wasn't sure what was best or appropriate.

Your mind works like a mainframe.

She could hear Michael Jeter's—head of the organization that had helped her develop her computer skills to the point of genius, and who had also made her life a living hell—voice in her head. But it was nothing short of the truth. She did think analytically, rationally and logically, just like a computer.

Not the way to help someone going through an emotional crisis.

Ironically, it had been her own emotions—feelings of inadequacy and incompetence—that had been blocking her mind from realizing the truth.

Tanner didn't need her to help him emotionally. He needed the part of her brain that worked like a computer. He needed her to help figure out the real killer so he could get back to the job he loved. Emotion had nothing to do with that.

As soon as it had become clear to her, she'd asked the Andrewses for the rest of the day off, and tomorrow as well. She'd gone home and grabbed the computer she generally tried to avoid, the one she hadn't touched since looking up details about owning a puppy last week.

It was time to work the problem. There was no one better at doing that than her.

Tanner turned from the wood he was chopping to look at her as she got out of the car. She tried not to swallow her tongue at the sight of him clad only in a cowboy hat and jeans—chest bare.

She was never going to get tired of looking at him. It was more than just his strong chin and carved jaw that already had a hint of shadow to it even at this hour. More than his broad, powerful shoulders that tapered into trim waist and hips. It was more than those deep brown eyes that seemed to notice everything.

It was all of it. The whole package put together that made up Tanner as a whole.

He walked toward her. She liked the way he walked. Not graceful. Not aggressive, but…powerful.

"You're home early," he said. "It's still midmorning."

She finally tore her eyes away from his torso to look up at his face. "Yeah. I brought pie. It's good at any time, even morning."

He reached over and tucked a strand of hair behind her ear. "Pie is a very distant second to the reason I'm glad you're here."

Her eyes dropped back to his naked chest. She wanted to close the inches that separated them and lick it.

She wanted to get them back to the passionate kisses where he slammed her against the wall. *That* kiss had been leading somewhere she desperately wanted to go.

But there hadn't been any kisses like that since he'd been suspended from the force.

The words were out of her mouth before she could stop them. "I want us to get back to the slamming against the wall, so I brought my computer." She grimaced. That hadn't come out the way she'd meant it to.

He chuckled. "You might have to throw in a little more information for me. I didn't quite follow your brain that time."

She decided to leave out the part about passionate kisses against the wall. Especially when she was a second and a half from licking his chest.

She took a breath. "You're frustrated about being suspended from the force. I can't help much with the emotional part, but I can help you with my computer and my mind."

His eyes narrowed. "Whitaker is on the case. He has experience with this sort of thing. He'll eventually get it figured out."

She rolled her eyes. "The same guy who thought I killed Newkirk? It could take him weeks just to figure out how to get his head out of his ass. I'll never get any more kisses if we're depending on him."

Tanner chuckled again and stepped closer. "I seem to recall kissing you this morning before you went to work."

Oh gosh, why did his sweat smell so good? So clean and male and *Tanner*. "I want the *other* kisses," she whispered. "Like the one before we went to your mom's house."

His brown eyes darkened, and his hand slid down to wrap around her waist, pulling her against him.

Every single part of her insides seemed to clench. *Yes.* This was what she wanted.

But before his lips touched hers, he seemed to withdraw back into himself. His fingers that had been grasping her waist with an almost bruising force a moment ago loosened.

He stepped back, rubbing his hand over his eyes. "Bree—"

She sighed. She'd become used to the distance between them. "I know. You're upset about what's happening, and doing romance with me is the last thing on your mind. That's okay. I—"

His mouth was on hers and she was backed up against the car—just like she'd been against the wall—before she knew what was going on. She gasped, and he took full advantage of it, thrusting deeply into her mouth with his tongue before withdrawing and coaxing hers to play. She sank into the kiss, her mind going blank as his lips ravished hers.

When he finally backed away, all she could do was stare at him.

"*Doing romance*, and doing a hell of a lot more, is always on my mind when it comes to you," he whispered. "Don't ever think I don't want to be around you any way I can get you, no matter what is going on with my job."

"O-okay."

They both stood there for many moments, breathing unsteadily.

"But I know how much your job means to you," she finally said. "And Risk Peak needs you back. So I want to help. Please let me help."

"What did you have in mind?"

She slid over and opened the car door, grabbing her laptop.

"You know I have a computer, right?" he asked. "You don't have to bring yours."

She shrugged. "This one is…better."

He shook his head, a half smile pulling at the corner of his mouth. "I'm not even going to ask."

"Probably a good idea."

He led her inside, and she sat down at the kitchen table, staring at her laptop.

Tanner stayed next to her as she breathed through her anxiety. Opening it up was tough. Her history with computers in a serious way—beyond researching puppy facts—was tied to being physically and emotionally tortured. She had to remind herself that the computer itself couldn't hurt her in any way.

"You okay?" he asked.

"I used it a few months ago when I helped bring down the Organization. This should be quite a bit easier than that."

He crouched down next to her so they were eye to eye. "You had to do that in order to save the world. You don't *have* to do this. I'll be just fine, you know.

Whitaker will eventually crack who really killed those two guys."

"No, I'm okay. I want to do this. The computer can't hurt me. Jeter can't hurt me anymore, either."

He reached over and kissed her knee. "That's the damn truth."

He straightened, and she opened the laptop, allowing it to boot. The first few keystrokes into her search were the most difficult, but then her brain let go of its fear and she dived in.

This was what she was most gifted at in the world.

Gaining access to the Colorado state system to find out more information about Peter Anders and Joshua Newkirk didn't take her long at all.

"I'm going to shower while you work. It's probably better if I don't know too much about what's going on here."

Her fingers continued to fly over the keyboard. "I'm not breaking any laws." *Yet.* "Have you been cutting wood since I left this morning?"

"No. Ironically, I had to go into the main sheriff's office earlier for a couple hours. I had an appointment I couldn't get out of." He paused. "With the police department psychiatrist."

Now her fingers stilled on the keys. "Oh. Because of being on suspension?"

"No. Something else. Something that happened a few years ago. Something you and I should probably talk about."

That didn't sound promising. She looked over at him. "Right now?"

"No. It's not something easily explained."

She nodded. "A complicated past is something I understand. So whenever you're ready."

He kissed the top of her head. "Thank you."

He walked off toward the shower, and Bree found herself staring at the screen without really seeing it. Mrs. Dempsey had been right. Tanner had demons—ones big enough to need required appointments with a psychiatrist years later.

Not that she thought less of him for seeing a psychiatrist. She was very aware she'd be much more emotionally well-adjusted if she'd been able to talk to someone about what she'd gone through.

It just…stung a little that she'd been living under the same roof as Tanner for almost a week—seeing him nearly daily for over a month—and he'd never mentioned an event traumatic enough to need psychiatric care.

What did it say that he hadn't felt like he could even mention that to her? Especially after everything she'd told him about her past.

Bree forced the thought aside. It would have to wait. She needed to focus on the mission in front of her now: discovering whatever she could about Anders and Newkirk. She started with all the legal ways she knew of gaining information and searching public records. Then slid into slightly more morally gray area, but still not technically illegal.

Both Anders and Newkirk had lived colorful and violent lives. Both had had run-ins with the law before they'd gotten arrested for the specific crimes they'd actually gone to jail for. But they didn't seem to have run in the same circles or have known the same people.

Both had spent time in prison, although they hadn't served at the same place at the same time. Both had gotten out of prison earlier than they should have, although Bree couldn't find out why without definitely crossing into the illegal-hacking area.

It was easy to see why Tanner was a suspect. As arresting officer, he definitely was the most obvious link between the two dead men.

It took Bree another two hours of searching—a pretty damn long time given her skills—before she finally found someone else in common. And even then it wasn't easy to spot.

Both Anders and Newkirk had been a cell mate of a Darin Carrico. Newkirk for six months. Anders for less than a week.

It was a weak tie, at best. But it was all Bree could find unless Tanner wanted her to really jump into illegal territory. She doubted he would be comfortable with morally gray, much less morally pitch-black.

Besides shoving a sandwich in front of her at lunch, Tanner had stayed out of her way. He knew what she was like when she was working—he'd seen her in action a few months ago. How focused she stayed. He hadn't bothered her.

She was filtering through sites and databases at a rapid clip and wanted to make sure not to miss anything. But as it became more and more evident she wasn't going to find much of anything online, she admitted that some relationships and associations didn't show up in a computer. Even ghosting through the men's social media accounts hadn't turned up anything to link the two of them. Sometimes there just wasn't a visible electronic trail, even for two people who knew each other.

And if she couldn't find anything except a weak tie to an old cell mate, she could damn well imagine nobody at the Grand County Sheriff's Department was going to find much.

She sighed. This did not mean good news for Tanner.

Chapter Twelve

An hour later Bree pushed back from the computer and turned to Tanner. "Okay, I've got bad news and worse news."

"That doesn't sound promising." Tanner held a hand out to her from where he sat on the couch. She stood and walked over to him, smiling as he grabbed her wrist and pulled her down next to him.

"There aren't very many overt ties between Newkirk and Anders. I've pretty much tapped out all legal channels. But if you'll just give the okay, I can—"

His fingers threaded through hers. "No. I don't want you breaking any laws. I didn't kill those men. The circumstances with how it went down were damn unfortunate, but they're not going to charge me. So, let's not do anything illegal."

She nodded. "Okay. Well, we do have one possibility. The only other connection I could find between Newkirk and Anders was that they were both cell mates, albeit very briefly, with a man named Darin Carrico."

"I don't recognize the name."

She stood, pulling Tanner with her over to the laptop at the table. With a couple of keystrokes, she had Carrico's arrest record pulled up.

"Darin Carrico, age twenty-five, arrested for trespassing, burglary and illegal sale of handguns as well as a long list of misdemeanors. He's been in prison for four years and has another three to go."

Tanner leaned over her shoulder to get a better look at Carrico's mug shot. "Yeah, I still don't recognize him."

"Newkirk was his cell mate for six months. Anders was his roomie for five nights."

Tanner let out an audible sigh. "That's a pretty thin connection."

"But it is something. And Carrico is currently incarcerated at Colorado Correctional Center. That's less than an hour away."

"I can't question him in any sort of official capacity. Not while I'm on suspension."

Bree spun around in her chair so she could face him. She'd already researched this, too. "But your badge could get us in, right? That's all we need. If we leave right now, we can catch him today. Otherwise we'll have to wait until this weekend. I know you can't ask him anything official, but at least we could see if he tips his hand in any way."

Maybe this would lead to nothing. Maybe Carrico had nothing to do with it. But if this was something that helped Tanner to feel like he was more in control of his own fate, then it was worth the drive.

It didn't take much to convince Tanner of the plan, and a little over an hour and a half later, they'd made it to Camp George West, the nickname for the Colorado Correctional Center. They were searched, signed in and waiting for Carrico at a table in the large visiting room.

"Why don't you let me do most of the talking," Tanner said, giving her hand a squeeze.

She rolled her eyes. "Do you really think I'm going to argue with you when you tell me I *don't* have to interact with someone else?"

He chuckled softly and leaned over to kiss her temple. "I guess not."

There was no recognition whatsoever in Carrico's face as a guard escorted him to the table. Since Colorado Correctional was a lower security level, Carrico wasn't in any sort of shackles. He did have on an unattractive orange jumpsuit that hung off his thin frame.

"You guys Jesus people?" Carrico asked as he sat down across from them at the table, his thin lips twisted in a sneer. "Because no offense, but I'm not interested."

"No," Tanner said. "My name is Tanner Dempsey, and this is Bree. We wanted to see if we could ask you a few questions about Joshua Newkirk and Peter Anders."

A dark, bitter look overtook Carrico's face, and he muttered a vile curse. "You're cops. Why the hell are you coming in here like you're visitors?"

Tanner shook his head. "I'm not here in any sort of official capacity. I'm just here to talk."

Carrico leaned back and crossed his arms over his chest. "But you are a cop, right, pig?"

Tanner just shrugged. "I work for the Grand County Sheriff's Department, yes."

"And why exactly should I help you?"

"All I want to know is whether you know Anders and Newkirk. That's all."

Carrico shook his head. "You obviously know that I was cell mates with both of them, or you wouldn't be here."

"You had any contact with them since they got out?"

"Yeah, we're pen pals. I get a perfume-scented letter once a week from both of them." Carrico rolled his eyes. "No, I haven't heard from either one of those bastards, not that I expected to. They weren't my friends. Although, if you run into either of them, ask them who the hell's ass they had to kiss to get their early release."

Bree wondered if Tanner would bring up that no one would be asking them anything since they were dead. That was probably what Bree would've blurted out. But he kept his cool. "Why? You looking to get out early?"

"You kidding me?" Carrico scoffed. "There's no way I think I'll get out early. I just want to stop your cop bastard friends from sending me to Colorado State Pen."

Tanner leaned closer to the table. "Why are you getting sent up to a level-three facility? You get into trouble here? A fight?"

"Hell, no. Look, man, I got a daughter. A little girl. I get to see her twice a week right now, but I won't ever get to see her at a supermax security. You can't take a kid in there. I'm just trying to do my time and get out, but somebody screwed me over."

Bree might not be good at reading interpersonal cues, but Carrico was visibly upset about being sent to this higher-security prison.

"You're in on nonviolent charges, right?" Tanner asked, eyes narrowing. "If you got sentenced here and you haven't done anything to merit being sent up, then there shouldn't be any reason why an appeal won't go through."

"Yeah, well, already tried that, and it didn't work. Somebody has it in for me, and I don't know who or why." Carrico slouched over on the table, smirk on his face. "Grand County, huh? I even talked to your department's shrink when he came here yesterday. Dr. Michael whatever. Thought for a minute he was going to help me, but shouldn't have gotten my hopes up."

Tanner sat up straight. "Wait—are you saying Dr.

Craig Michalski was here yesterday? He came to see you?"

"Yep."

Tanner glanced at Bree before turning back to Carrico. Holy crap. Was Michalski the same department psychiatrist Tanner had gone to see this morning? Had Michalski realized the connection between Carrico and the two murder victims? If so, he obviously hadn't mentioned it to Tanner at their appointment.

"What did he say to you?" Tanner asked.

"You both work for the same department. Why don't you ask him?"

Tanner's lips pressed together to a thin line. "Was he asking about Anders and Newkirk?"

"Dude, nobody cares about your boyfriends but you." Carrico turned to Bree. "Honey, he obviously isn't giving you what you need. Sorry I can't help you from in here, but I know some people if you're looking for real men who know how to treat a woman right."

Her skin crawled, and she shrank back into herself as Carrico leered at her. Tanner's palm slammed down on the table. "Eyes on me, jackass."

Carrico held out his hands in front of him in a gesture of—obviously false—submission. "Sorry, Officer."

Tanner visibly got himself under control. "Why don't you tell me what Dr. Michalski was here to talk to you about and I will look into why they are moving you into a higher-security prison. No promises, but if there's been some sort of mistake, I can help rectify that. I can make sure you stay here, where you can have visits with your daughter."

Carrico snorted. "You know what? I don't believe for one second that you're really going to help me. You cops ain't done nothing but screw me over. But you know what? I'll try, just in case—"

"Carrico." A guard walked over, interrupting them. "You've got a visitor. That okay, Deputy, or you want us to have him wait?"

Tanner nodded and a few moments later a man who looked almost exactly like Carrico, except more skinny—hard to believe that was even possible—and pale, walked over to their table. If Bree had been asked which one was in prison just based on looks she would've said this new guy, who was obviously Carrico's brother. Carrico's *sickly and pale* brother.

"Who the hell is this?" the guy asked as he reached over and squeezed Carrico's shoulder.

"This would be Grand County officer of the law Dempsey, and his lady friend."

The new man's eyes narrowed. "Why are you here?"

"Who are you?" Tanner asked.

"I'm Glen, Darin's brother. I'm here twice a week to see him. I don't think you can say the same."

"No. I'll be honest—before this afternoon I wasn't even aware Darin existed. I'm here, completely off duty, to ask him about Joshua Newkirk and Peter Anders."

Glen shook his head. "God, you cops are all the same. Always taking, never giving. You're about to send my brother up to a max security prison. Why the hell should he help you with a damn thing?"

"I've already made my offer to Darin to look into it. I can't make any promises, but maybe there's something that can be done."

Glen just turned to his brother. "Darin, no. We've heard this before. No more help to these bastards until they help you first." The pale man spun to stare at Tanner and Bree. "My brother's done talking to you. Don't come back here. Or I'll be filing a complaint on my brother's behalf."

Tanner stood and Bree stood with him. Tanner turned to Darin. "If you change your mind, look me up. Tanner Dempsey. You have my word that I'll look into this, even if you can't help me with my questions."

Carrico shrugged. "Well, like I said, if Anders or Newkirk have some words of wisdom about who to talk to about stopping this transfer, I'd be glad to hear it."

Tanner said nothing, just led Bree out with a hand at the small of her back.

"Well, that was a bust. Sorry," she said as he opened the door for her and she climbed into the passenger seat.

"Not totally."

"Because you think he might talk to you? Glen was going to allow that over his dead body, which, admittedly, looked like it might be relatively soon."

Tanner shook his head. "No, I doubt I'll hear from him."

"Then how did it help?"

"Well, for one, Darin definitely didn't recognize me when he first saw me. Didn't know my name."

Bree nodded. "Yeah, he would have to be one hell of an actor if he did."

"Also, I don't think Darin knows Newkirk and Anders are dead. Admittedly, he could be playing us, but I honestly don't think he wanted anything more but to ask them who could keep him from going to Colorado State Penitentiary." He scrubbed a hand across his face. "Not that any of this is going to help me get reinstated."

She hated that Tanner looked even more defeated as he started the car and pulled out of the parking area. She'd really wanted this to make a difference.

He grabbed her hand and pulled it up to his lips. "Thank you for bringing us out here. Even if Darin has nothing to do with what's going on with me, somebody still needs to look into what's going on with him, because the situation doesn't sound right. So good comes out of this no matter what."

Bree's heart gave a little tug. That he would be up to his eyeballs in his own problems and was still going to make it a priority to find justice even for a criminal…

How the heck was she supposed to keep herself from falling in love with him?

Chapter Thirteen

They got back to the ranch and ate dinner, but Bree wasn't done looking into this. If there was one thing all her experience with computer coding had taught her, it was that when the coding led to a dead end, you had to step back until you could find a way around whatever had trapped you.

Carrico seemed to be a dead end, but maybe Bree just needed to find a way around him and see if anything else was there. Perhaps the guy was just what he appeared to be: someone who wanted not to be sent to a supermax prison so he could continue to receive visits from his daughter.

But Bree had spent a big chunk of her life within an organization that had fooled the entire world into thinking they were good and altruistic, when really they were emotionless, sadistic bastards.

Tanner was a good man who wanted to believe the best of everyone. He got that from his parents. Bree had heard the story of how his father had been killed in the line of duty because he'd trusted someone who had then shot him.

She didn't think Tanner was gullible in any way, shape or form. But she was going to look more closely at Carrico before giving him the benefit of the doubt. Research him impartially and dispassionately to make sure he was truly a dead end and not involved in all of this somehow.

And she wasn't afraid to bend a few laws to do it, regardless of Tanner's opinion.

Her emotional stuntedness was working to her advantage in this case. She didn't give a rat's ass about Carrico's sob story if it meant clearing Tanner's name.

A couple of hours later, she was glad she'd stayed the course, despite Tanner's repeated attempts to get her to put away the computer for the night.

When she found it, she could barely believe her eyes.

"Tanner, I found something."

He looked up from whatever type of sporting event he was watching. Football, maybe? She wasn't good with sports.

"I don't even know what you've been looking for the past two hours."

"I think our friend Carrico may not be as innocent as we thought."

Tanner flipped off the television and walked over to her. "What makes you say that?"

This was where it got a little bit tricky. "Because Carrico is currently in a lower-security prison, he has access to email. It's monitored, but he sent a message to two separate guerrilla mail accounts—which are temporary and completely anonymous addresses—one eight nights ago and one four nights ago."

"The nights before Anders and Newkirk were killed."

Bree nodded.

"What did the emails say?"

"The first one said, Last fall the beautiful flowers made me smile although they soon withered and flew away. The second, Every laugh makes me think of pudding."

"Okay, definitely weird. But the messages don't sound suspicious or dangerous to me."

Bree had recognized the foursquare cipher as soon as she'd read the email. It had taken her a little while to break it, but not very long. "There's a code. A cipher."

Now she had his full attention. "You're sure?"

She turned the screen so he could see the words the highlighted code provided.

Newkirk tomorrow.

She scrolled down so he could see the other one: Anders ASAP.

Tanner let out a low curse. "Who did those messages go to? Is there any way of finding that out?"

"The proxy is anonymous, so I can't get much more information without significantly more illegal effort, and even then it's iffy. It's an anonymous, en- crypted email that uses a VPN to reroute and hide the IP address. Sites like these are utilized when people are trying to be…covert."

He collapsed down in the chair next to her, still staring at the screen. "Covert. In other words, il- legal."

"Not always. Maybe they're cheating on a spouse or something. But yeah, illegal in this case. I know the words themselves don't prove anything…"

"But the fact that they were sent within hours of both men being killed, and that Carrico knew both of them, is significant. More damning than what they have on me."

She smiled. "That's what I thought, too. That's good, right?"

"It's definitely a start." His eyes narrowed as he looked at her more closely. "You said we can't get the other email without you being *more* illegal? That means even getting this much was illegal."

She shrugged. "Yeah. But just a little. And if it leads us to the real killer then who cares, right?"

"A judge is going to care."

She cringed. She wasn't used to thinking about things like judges. "You don't have to give the sheriff's department specifics, just point them in the right direction. Even Whitaker couldn't be dumb enough to miss this if it's staring him in the face."

He laughed, and it sounded more carefree and

Tanner-like than she'd heard most of the week. Her heart did another tumble.

He brushed a finger down her cheek. "Damn it, woman. What am I going to do with you?"

His hand reached into the hair at her nape, and he pulled her into his lap with a quick tug. She hardly let out a little laugh of her own before his mouth was on hers.

The kiss started out light, playful, with Bree draped over the back of one of his arms and the other moving in gentle circles on her hip. But before long the kiss turned much hotter and demanding.

The needs in her body were hot and demanding, too.

She wanted Tanner.

She hooked an arm around his neck, pulling him closer, deepening the kiss herself, not that he seemed to mind. When his lips moved down her jaw to her neck, she couldn't stop the moan that fell from her lips.

She hadn't even known it was possible to feel this way. Like everything was on fire and burning and there was nothing more she wanted than to be consumed by the flame.

Tanner wrapped one of his big arms around her waist and stood, raising them both easily with his strength, and took a step toward the bedroom.

Finally.

She wrapped her legs around his hips, her arms clasped tightly around his neck as his lips moved back to hers. Keeping her pressed against him as he walked.

He slowed momentarily as he moved them through the bedroom door, and she tensed. She didn't want him to stop. She felt like she'd been waiting for this her entire life.

She brought her lips back to his, kissing him deeper. It was the only way she could think of to let him know without words how much she wanted this. She threaded her fingers into his thick dark hair and kept their mouths fused.

Whatever it was she was trying to communicate, Tanner understood. His fingers on her hips gripped her closer—strong, secure, confident.

She knew he would take her wherever she wanted to go.

A FEW HOURS LATER, Bree woke up. She stretched, not even for one second trying to keep the smile off her face.

She'd had no idea.

No idea that two people could be as close as she and Tanner had just been. The things that lawman could do with his hands and lips ought to be illegal.

And was she supposed to have known that there were spots on her body—*innocent* spots on her body— that he could use against her so succinctly?

The backs of her knees.

The spot just below her ear.

Her navel.

And he'd found—and paid attention to—every single freckle she had.

She was never, *ever* going to be able to look at her body the same way after what they'd done.

And they hadn't even had sex, technically. When Tanner had laid her on the bed and told her there was a lot more he wanted to show her tonight that didn't include intercourse, she'd been skeptical. Thought it was just another way he was trying to keep distance from her.

She'd been so wrong. He'd definitely not been trying to keep his distance from her.

Afterward, he'd carried her exhausted, sated body into the shower. The water had perked her up a little, and she'd convinced him to show her what *he* liked.

It was only after the hot water started to run out that they'd finally left the shower. Tanner had dried them both off and tucked her body next to him in the bed, turning out the light.

Curled up next to him, she'd drifted off to sleep cognizant that she'd never thought she'd ever have this sort of intimacy with someone, much less someone she cared about as much as Tanner. Never thought she would feel as cherished as she did right in that moment. She'd fallen asleep happier than she'd ever been, Tanner wrapped around her like her own personal blanket.

But when she reached over for him in the bed now just a few hours later, he wasn't there.

She waited a couple of minutes to make sure he

hadn't just gone to the bathroom, but it didn't take her long to realize that wasn't the case.

She glanced over at the clock. It was almost 4:00 a.m., too early for him to be out doing any chores or getting ready for work. Maybe he'd gotten hungry. She grinned again. They'd certainly burned enough calories. She wouldn't mind a bite to eat herself.

But when she came out of the bedroom, she found him asleep on the couch. And not just in the accidentally-sat-down-and-fell-back-asleep stance. He had taken out a pillow and a blanket and made himself a little bed.

Away from her.

"Tanner?"

He'd been a cop for too long to wake up groggy. Even in the dim light, she could see awareness in his eyes. "You okay, freckles?"

"Why are you out here sleeping rather than in the bedroom with me?"

Suddenly everything she'd been feeling—all the closeness and intimacy she'd been celebrating—melted away. Obviously, he didn't feel the same connection between them, or he wouldn't have come out to the couch to sleep as soon as he could untangle himself from her.

He shook his head. "Whatever you're thinking, stop. This isn't what it looks like."

She wrapped her arms around her middle, trying to fortify herself. "It looks like you were sleeping out here rather than sleeping with me. Is that not the case?"

He let out a sigh. "Yes, but not because I didn't want to be next to you. Believe me, there is nothing more I wanted than to sleep with you tucked against me, especially after the things we just did together."

Honestly, she wasn't sure whether to believe him or not. Tanner wasn't a liar. She knew that down to the very marrow of her bones.

But years of insecurity and knowing how bad she could be at interpersonal situations ate at her. All the possible mistakes she could've made and not even have been aware of it.

"Did I do something wrong?" she whispered. Except for in the shower, she'd definitely been more on the receiving end of pleasure than the giving end. "Was I too selfish? I didn't do enough for you?"

He flew off the couch and pulled her into his arms. "No, Bree. Hell, nothing like that. It was amazing for me. *All* of it—especially watching you come apart in my arms like that—was amazing for me."

She could hear his heartbeat under her ear, but it didn't reassure her the way it had when he'd pulled her against him a few hours ago.

The urge to flee was overwhelming. To get away and be by herself. It was so hard to feel like she'd grown so much only to see herself spiral back down into the need to run.

But maybe that would be the best thing. "Look, I should probably go. Maybe stay at my house since everything seems to be working out for you professionally-wise."

His hands came up to cup her cheeks, tilting her head back until she was forced to look at him. God, looking at him right now was so hard.

"No. No more running. I want you here. I want you with me."

She sucked in her breath. "I don't understand."

He kissed her forehead. "Just give me a chance to explain it to you, and if you still want to leave, then I won't stop you."

Chapter Fourteen

Tanner wanted to kick his own ass. He'd just experienced the greatest night of his entire life—bar *none*—and now he had made Bree feel like she'd done something wrong.

He looked down into her green eyes that seemed so wary and guarded now. He would go the rest of his life making sure he never put that look in her eyes again.

He was thirty-three years old and hadn't lived like a monk. He knew what had just happened between him and Bree in the last few hours had been special. It had been the type of connection many people searched for their whole lives, but few ever found.

Tanner wanted to spend the rest of his life getting to know all the nooks and crannies of this woman's body. Find every single place his lips could touch that made her gasp, sigh or moan. And then stick around those places until she was calling out his name.

But he couldn't do that until she knew the truth.

"I suffer from night terrors. Sometimes I wake

up and think I'm trapped in a situation somewhere else, and I come out swinging."

He knew enough about Bree to know that cutting right to the heart of it was the best way to communicate with her. She was never going to be one for subtlety or sugarcoating.

Even now he could see her mind trying to turn over the facts and put them in their proper place. "You were afraid you would hurt me."

He smiled. Of course she came to the correct assumption immediately. She was brilliant. But then his smile faded. He trailed the back of his knuckles down her cheek. "Yes. You've already been through so much violence, freckles, I didn't want to add to your burden. I couldn't stand the thought that I could hurt you coming out of my nightmares and make you afraid of me."

She sighed and nodded. "We'll come back to that. Can you tell me specifically what causes the night terrors, or is it something more general?"

He could almost see her mentally making a checklist of things to research.

A slight shiver shook her frame, since she was nearly naked in the cold living room. He reached down and snagged the blanket off the couch, wrapping it around her. Then he picked her up, blanket and all, and sat down with her in his lap. He *needed* her to be close just as much as he *wanted* to be close to her.

"It's PTSD from an undercover case gone impossibly wrong three years ago."

She listened in intense Bree fashion as he explained about the Viper Syndicate. How he'd been discovered as undercover, and Nate Fletcher and Alex Peterson had also been with him. He left out a lot of the gory details of his physical beating and torture. She didn't need to know that. She'd lived through enough of her own horrific violence. But telling her about how it all ended? The nightmares that still plagued him? That, he owed her.

"They were trying to force me to tell them if I was working with someone else. I figured there was no way I was walking out of there alive, so I might as well not take down two other good men with me."

He felt her arms wrap around him through the blanket. He tucked her head more firmly under his chin and forced himself to tell the rest of the story.

"SWAT raided the building and spooked the Vipers. They killed the first officer, Alex Peterson, immediately." He sucked in a breath. "I broke the noose around my neck and was diving for the guy about to execute Nate Fletcher, but I was too late."

She sat quietly for a long time, her arms wrapped around him like she would fight anything or anyone that dared to want to harm him. "The night terrors… What are they about mostly? Being strangled? Being helpless?"

Tanner closed his eyes and breathed in the scent of her. She understood. Maybe more than anybody else he'd ever talked to about this, because of her own experiences. She'd probably suffered from night terrors herself after what she'd been through.

"All of it. The pain, the fear, but mostly my inability to save Nate. If I had just broken that noose sooner. Just found the strength to do that, it might've been enough. A young man with his whole life in front of him might still be here."

"Or you might have died right along with him. It's like what you told me about what Michael Jeter did to my mother. We can only make the best choices we have in the circumstances we are in." She rubbed her chin against his chest. "I know that doesn't make it any easier to take. But I know if you could go back right now and save Fletcher's life, even at the cost of your own, you would do it. There's something to be said for that."

How many times had Dr. Michalski tried to tell him the same thing? That Tanner had done the best he could in the situation he was in. That maybe he could've broken that rope around his neck sooner, but there was no guarantee it would've made any difference whatsoever.

Tanner didn't blame the SWAT team for not coming in two minutes earlier, so why was it okay to blame himself?

He understood that; he really did. But at the end of the day, like Ryan Fletcher had pointed out, Nate wasn't around to celebrate his twenty-fifth birthday this year.

"The night terrors have been worse this week because of my frustration about the murders and being suspended," he said. "Believe me, I wanted to be with you in every way a man can be with a woman, but I don't want to hurt you further."

She nodded and let out a breath. "I know I'm not good with emotional stuff. I'm never going to be good with emotional stuff."

"Freckles—"

She kissed his chest. "No, let me finish."

He shut up and kept his arms around her. "I'm not good at the emotional stuff, but I'm not weak, Tanner. My past may have been brutal, but it made me strong. I know you and I haven't really talked about exactly where we are going with our relationship."

He wanted to stop right there. Wanted to explain to her that, especially after earlier tonight, he was all in.

All. In.

There was nothing he wanted more than to spend the rest of his life with this woman. But he was older than her by nearly a decade. He had seen and done so much more than she'd been able to do, living on the run most of her life. He was willing to take however long she needed—to wait forever—for her to feel ready to start a life with him.

"You've been so patient with me," she continued. "Taking things slow and going at a pace I'm comfortable with. And I so appreciate your willingness to do that."

Now he had to stop her. "Because you're worth it." He kissed the top of her head. He meant every word.

She squeezed him then moved back so they could look eye to eye. "It means the world that you think so. And I feel the same. But if we are ever going to go forward as a true couple, you've got to know that *I don't break.* At least, not very easily."

She was right, of course. He'd been doing them both a disservice by hiding this from her. Keeping it a secret had forced him to carry too much and insulted her by implying she wasn't strong enough to help lift his burden.

He reached down and framed her face with both hands. "I've never thought you anything but incredibly strong. But what I did was downright stupid, and you're right to call me on it."

The tiniest of smiles lit up her face. "I don't get to do that with you very often, Captain Dempsey. You're a pretty smart guy. But I want to help you. We can work out your triggers together. And hell, if I take a shot to the jaw from you in the middle of a night terror, you'll just owe me one."

He raised an eyebrow. "You mean you'll want a return shot to my jaw?"

"No. But after the last few hours, I can think of *many* different ways for you to work off any guilt. And we haven't even gotten to the really interesting stuff yet. Imagine what I can come up with once you teach me how sex really works."

She shifted so she was straddling his lap. There was nothing separating them but the thin blanket.

She grinned, and that beautiful smile was all woman. Tanner felt his heart tumble over into an abyss he knew he was never coming back from.

He gave her his own smile. "You know, for someone who feels like she doesn't know how to say the right things, you do a pretty damn good job."

Because she had. Just by being Bree, she had shifted some of the weight he carried. Helped disseminate it more evenly between the two of them.

They were a team. And he was head-over-ass in love with this woman.

"Good. You won't break me, Tanner. I promise."

He kissed her. He meant it to be a kiss of reverence and thanks. But it soon turned into something much more passionate.

"I think we better head back to the bedroom and practice some of those apology moves, just in case you need them. Especially the ones that involve you kissing right here." She pointed to the spot on the side of her neck just below her ear.

"I've created a monster."

Wrapping his hands under her hips, he stood and carried her back into the bedroom. He'd be kissing her there and a lot of other places. And when they fell asleep afterward, he'd be right there by her side, where he belonged.

Chapter Fifteen

Bree rode with Tanner to the sheriff's office in the northern part of Grand County the next morning. She still had the day off work and wanted to be there in case Whitaker was too oblivious to see what was right in front of his ass.

She offered to write it down for Tanner in case he needed a direct quote.

Tanner had no intention of allowing Bree to admit any illegal doings to Whitaker. He didn't trust the man not to lose sight of the bigger picture—finding the murderer—and arrest Bree just out of spite.

It would take a while for Whitaker to follow up on everything Tanner would present. Tanner didn't expect to be reinstated today, although he was hoping the wheels would be turning enough that maybe he'd be back tomorrow.

But today both he and Bree had the day off. Too bad it was cold and rainy out, or else he'd spend it convincing Bree to move in with him permanently at the ranch and hauling the rest of her stuff.

He wanted her there. He'd never met someone who belonged at the ranch and loved it as much as he and Noah. If it were up to Tanner, Bree wouldn't spend another night away from him for the rest of their lives.

So much for trying to take it slow for her sake. At least he hadn't dragged her off in front of a county judge to get married.

The thought had crossed his mind.

"What do you want to do today?" she asked, smiling over at him from the passenger seat. "My vote is for going back to bed and—"

She gasped and gripped the door handle as a car cut in front of them on the rainy road, way too close.

Tanner let out a low curse. Not only had the guy cut him off, he was now hitting his brakes. Tanner slowed down, then tried to go around him, but the guy swerved again so they were trapped behind him.

"What the hell?" Tanner muttered.

The driver continued to tap his brakes, forcing Tanner to slow further behind him. He flipped on his blinker and pulled to the side of the road. Tanner pulled off also.

He reached over into the glove compartment and pulled out his backup firearm that he had a concealed-carry permit to keep inside his vehicle.

"What just happened?" Bree's green eyes were huge.

"Stay here. I'm going to talk to this guy and see what the hell is going on."

He reached over and gave her hand a squeeze before opening the car door and stepping outside. At least the rain had reduced itself into a mist.

The door of the car in front of him opened and Tanner stopped, firearm ready but pointed at the ground. Then Tanner saw who it was.

"Ryan?" Tanner relaxed his grip on the gun. "You nearly gave me a heart attack. Why the hell did you almost run us off the road?"

Even through the low light and heavy mist, Tanner could see the tension radiating through Ryan Fletcher. It was unlike the lawyer to be so discombobulated. Every time Tanner had seen him in the courtroom, he'd been completely unflappable.

"Tanner, thank God I caught you. Sorry for the vehicular dramatics. I just didn't know how else to get in touch with you."

Tanner tucked his Glock into the back waistband of his jeans. "How about a telephone. That would work."

"I couldn't call. There couldn't be any trace of a call."

Now Tanner was getting concerned. "What's going on?"

"You can't go in to the sheriff's office. They're going to arrest you."

Tanner shook his head. "No, it's all been taken care of. We found some other evidence. Doesn't clear me outright, but it at least provides another link between the two dead guys besides me."

"I just came from Sheriff Duggan's office. Now there are *three* dead guys. Another body showed up this morning. Stabbed in the back again."

Damn it. "Well, I have a pretty ironclad alibi for last night." Bree would be able to provide a statement that he'd been with her for the entire night.

He rubbed his hand over his face. Except she *wouldn't* be able to attest to that in all honesty, would she? She had no idea how long he was gone from the bed before she came out and found him on the couch. She'd be willing to say he'd been in bed with her all night, but there was no way he was going to allow her to lie and commit perjury for him for that.

Tanner gritted his teeth. "I'm assuming this third victim is tied to me also, if they are threatening to get a warrant?"

"They've already got the warrant, Tanner. Judge issued it immediately based on the evidence. And the guy is tied to you and me both. Owen Duquette."

Tanner's curse was low and foul. "I wanted that bastard in prison, but I didn't kill him."

Ryan ran his hand through his hair. "Look, I'm not going to be shedding any tears over Duquette's death. Honestly, if you *did* kill him, I'm not even sure I would care, after how he was tied to Nate's death. But I don't think you did, and that's why I'm here."

He heard the car door open and held his hand out to Bree without even looking behind him. This affected her, too.

"Is everything okay?" she asked.

He pulled her to his side. "Bree, this is Ryan Fletcher. He works in the district attorney's office."

"Fletcher?" she asked softly.

Tanner nodded. "Nate Fletcher's brother."

Ryan stepped forward and held out his hand. "Nice to meet you. Sorry it's under these circumstances."

"What circumstances?"

Tanner wrapped an arm around her shoulders. "There's been another murder. Somebody else connected to me."

Bree's curse echoed his from a moment ago. "I don't understand what the hell is going on."

"When it was just Anders and Newkirk, I was willing to accept that it was a nasty coincidence. But three people tied to me?"

"This is some sort of setup," Ryan finished for him.

"I'm not big on conspiracy theories, but three dead guys that I arrested? That I lobbied pretty hard to keep in jail and am on record for being frustrated when they were let out? That's really starting to look like pretty good motive." Tanner scrubbed a hand down his face.

"But motive shouldn't be enough. Not for someone like you who has a stellar reputation in law enforcement," Bree said.

Ryan nodded. "She's right. Nobody would think about trying to arrest you based just on potential motive, even if it was good."

Tanner wasn't so sure. Whitaker didn't seem to need much more than that to be convinced of his guilt.

"But there's more than just motive," Ryan continued. "Your DNA was present at Duquette's crime scene. It was also present in Anders's car and at Newkirk's body."

"I've already admitted to being in Anders's car, and I was first on scene at Newkirk's death, so that would explain both of those. But I definitely haven't been anywhere near Duquette since he got out of prison."

The three of them looked at each other, the truth unavoidable. Someone was trying to frame Tanner for murder.

"Who would do this?" Bree whispered.

He wrapped his arm more tightly around her. "I don't know. But I'll talk to the sheriff, and we'll start gathering some possibilities. She and I have known each other for a long time. She worked for my dad. She'll give me the benefit of the doubt."

"Sheriff Duggan may not have that luxury," Ryan said. "I was at her office first thing this morning, because I got a call directly from the governor. Evidently, there's some concern that the sheriff may not be able to consider you objectively."

Tanner and Bree both cursed. Tanner had to smile when hers was quite a bit more colorful and descriptive.

But Ryan didn't have anything to smile about. "I

just came from a meeting with the sheriff, Whitaker and Dr. Michalski."

"Let me guess. Whitaker was the one leading the charge for my arrest."

Ryan rolled his eyes. "Actually, he seemed excited that there was *real* police action going on. It was Dr. Michalski who provided the most damning information. He overheard us talking after court last week. Remembered you saying Duquette would get what was coming to him."

Tanner threw up his hands. "As in, put back in jail as soon as he broke the law again, not murdering him."

"The sheriff asked Dr. Michalski point-blank if he thought you were capable of killing someone. Michalski said yes."

"*I'm* capable of killing someone," Bree muttered. "Actually, I don't have to kill them. I can just get into a computer system and make their entire identity—"

Tanner lifted his hand off her shoulder and wrapped it over her mouth. Ryan was his friend, but he was also the district attorney.

"She didn't get a lot of sleep last night. Just ignore her."

He shot her a warning look then removed his hand, a little afraid she might bite him. But she kept quiet.

"Look, your worst problem is your DNA showing up at Duquette's murder scene. Psych opinions and possible motive play a very distant second fiddle to that. I don't have all the details. I was just trying to get out of the sheriff's office and to your ranch so that I could warn you. If you go into that building right now, you're not coming back out a free man. Not today, at least."

Tanner hated the look of fear in Bree's eyes. "He's right," she whispered.

Tanner shook his head. "I've worked in law enforcement for a decade. My dad did for twice as long. I trust the system. It's not perfect, but it works, by and large."

"Unless you have someone working that system against you." Bree's small hand squeezed his. "I spent a good chunk of my life running from people who used the system against me."

"I'm not telling you to run," Ryan said. "As far as anybody in Grand County thinks, you don't know anything about this. Why don't you go off grid? A lovers' getaway, where no one can get in touch with you. Use that time to see if you can discover further information. I'll do the same."

Damn it. Tanner didn't want to run. It only made him look guilty.

"You can do a lot more for yourself out of a cell than you can inside one," Ryan continued. "Whoever is doing this has a pretty big reach. If you're inside, you're leaving others unprotected." His eyes shot to Bree.

She immediately shook her head. "No, I can take care of myself. I've been taking care of myself for a lot of years. If you feel the best thing is to turn your-self in right now, you should do that. I'll be doing what I can to help you from out here."

Which would undoubtedly be illegal.

While he had no doubt that Bree could and would take care of herself, he'd made her a promise a few months ago that she was no longer in this—in *life*—on her own. That was doubly true after last night.

Ryan was risking a significant amount by try-ing to warn Tanner. Tanner didn't take that lightly. The man could lose his job or even go to jail for ob-structing justice.

He was being given a gift. A head start on figuring out who was hunting him. He'd be a fool not to take it.

"Okay, I won't go in. For forty-eight hours, seventy-two at most, just to try to get a bead on who's after me."

The hunter was about to become the hunted.

Chapter Sixteen

"We need to go to my apartment," Bree said from inside the SUV as they watched Ryan pull back onto the road. "This SUV is too conspicuous, not to mention they probably have some sort of means of tracking it."

Tanner looked a little like he was in shock. She knew he wasn't one hundred percent on board with this decision to run. But if they didn't get moving right now, the option was going to be taken out of their hands.

Running, keeping away from people who were looking for you, was definitely in Bree's wheelhouse. God knew she had enough experience at it.

Tanner was still staring out the windshield into the rain.

She reached over and squeezed his hand. "Dempsey, let's go. Get safe first, fall apart later."

Yep, she'd just quoted her mother.

Tanner gave a brief nod then pulled onto the road and drove toward Risk Peak. Thank goodness they'd dropped her car off here yesterday on the way to the prison. They were going to need it and what she had in her apartment.

"I'm not even sure where we should go." Tanner's knuckles were white as he gripped the steering wheel.

"We're going to my apartment first. I have some things that will help us."

And at least they still had her computer with them. They were going to need that most of all.

She put a call in to Cheryl and Dan at the Sunrise Diner to let them know she wouldn't be in for a couple more days. She told them that Tanner had kidnapped her and taken her somewhere secluded and romantic, and she wasn't even exactly sure where she was.

She felt a little bit guilty at how excited they seemed at the thought. But Ryan was probably right. The best thing she and Tanner could do right now was make it seem like they had a reason to be out of pocket. And *not* look like they were on the run from the law.

She half expected Tanner to change his mind and decide to turn himself over to the sheriff, and fight this head-on. If he did, she wouldn't try to stop him or discourage him in any way.

Head-on was Tanner's way. And it was one of the things she loved most about him.

But he didn't. As a matter of fact, the closer they got to Risk Peak, the faster he drove, like he realized that they needed to get the hell out of Dodge quick.

"We won't have very long before they have an APB out on me. We've got to be out of town by then. They're going to be able to trace things like credit cards and ATMs, and I don't have that much cash on me."

"I've got everything we need in my apartment. Get me there, give me five minutes, maybe even less, and we can be on the road."

She'd struggled with the fact that she still had a bug-out bag packed and waiting in the corner of her closet, even though the Organization wasn't hunting her anymore. She told herself it made her a coward to keep it around, that it encouraged the bad habit of running when she got scared. But she hadn't been able to force herself to get rid of it.

And now she was glad.

Ten minutes later they were pulling up in front of her apartment.

She handed him the key to her car. "Grab anything useful from in here, and definitely my computer. I'll meet you at my car in five minutes."

He looked at her, expression tight. He was still white-knuckling the steering wheel. "You're running again. I never wanted you to be forced to do that. And now I'm dragging you into breaking the law with me."

He was about to be arrested for murder, and he was worried about *her*.

"We haven't actually seen the warrant out for your arrest, so technically we're not breaking any laws yet. Let's run away for a romantic getaway, just the two of us." She smiled. This was so much harder for him than it was for her.

He hit his palm against the steering wheel. "Fine. Three days, that's it. If we haven't figured out who's behind it by then, I'm turning myself in, back from our *romantic getaway*."

"Deal." If they didn't have any further info in three days, they were in a lot of trouble anyway.

"And when this is over, I'm taking you for a *real* romantic getaway, off grid, just the two of us."

She grinned. "Making an honest woman out of me—I like that."

"Trust me, if I'm not starting a thirty-year prison sentence in the next few months, I plan to make an honest woman out of you in every possible way."

She only got a second to gape at him before his fingers twisted in her hair at the nape of her neck—the way he seemed to like to do so much—and he pulled her in for a quick kiss. "Go get your magic bag of tricks. We don't have a lot of time."

"Three and a half minutes at my car." She was out the door without another word.

The bug-out bag was exactly where she'd left it. Thankful for the preparation and evasion skills her mother had instilled in her, even though they'd been so painful at the time, Bree grabbed it. It wasn't meant for two people, but it would give them a much better head start than law enforcement would be expecting.

Her phone buzzed in her purse. She took it out and looked at it.

Ronnie Kitchens. The deputy who worked with Tanner every day in Risk Peak.

Bree knew better than to answer it. She left the phone on her kitchen table and hefted the large back-pack onto her shoulder. They'd be coming here soon looking for her and Tanner. *Accidentally* leaving her phone would give credence to their claim that they were on a romantic getaway.

And she would not, under any circumstances, think about Tanner's comment about making an honest woman out of her. She needed to focus on getting them through this situation and keeping Tanner out of jail.

Not focusing on what it would be like to become Mrs. Bree Dempsey.

She was back out of her car with a few seconds to spare on her three and a half minutes. Tanner was already there, looking more grim. "Ronnie just called me."

She got in and he started the car. "You didn't answer, did you?"

"No. I'm sure he wants to know why there's an arrest warrant with my name on it coming across his desk."

"He called me, too. I left my phone on the table, so it will just look like I forgot it."

Tanner handed her his phone. "Do whatever you need to make sure they can't track me with this."

She ran her fingers along his old-fashioned flip phone. The fact that he didn't have a smartphone was what had saved her life a few months ago. She opened the back panel and removed the battery and the SIM card. It was doubtful they could've traced it, even as a whole unit, but keeping these pieces separate would definitely stop them.

She dropped the separate pieces into the cup holder in the console of her late-model gray Honda. It was one of the most popular cars in the United States, which was precisely why she owned it. This vehicle would blend in with every other car on the highway.

"Got any particular direction you think we should head?" he asked.

"Just out of Risk Peak, definitely not in the direction of the ranch, and probably not toward any of your family's houses, either."

He nodded. "Yes, those will be the first places they'll look."

They drove toward Denver, deciding that the more vehicles around, the less conspicuous they would be. As they approached Aurora, a suburb just outside Denver, they started running low on gas.

"We're going to have to stop," Tanner said. "But we can't run any credit cards. I have eighty-seven dollars in my wallet. That's not going to get us far."

"That's okay. I have about two thousand in my backpack."

He nearly gave himself whiplash as he spun to

look at her before returning his eyes to the road. "Why the hell do you have two thousand dollars in your backpack?"

She shrugged. "It's my bug-out bag. Do you know what that is?"

"I was raised in Colorado and have a brother who's always one step away from disappearing. So yeah, I know what a bug-out bag is. But most people have camping supplies and waterproof matches. Not two grand."

The term *bug-out bag* had been coined by survivalists to mean a bag that contained whatever emergency gear someone kept available and ready to go at a moment's notice—in case they needed to *bug out*. Most people thought of it in terms of wilderness survival.

Bree's bag was completely different. It did have some traditional supplies—a Mylar blanket, changes of clothes and a small first-aid kit. But Bree had never planned to be heading to the wilderness if she had to survive on the run. Her kit was for *urban* survival.

"Actually, I have something we should probably use now that we've cleared Risk Peak. Can you pull over at that rest stop ahead?"

Tanner nodded tightly and did as she asked. He definitely didn't look any more relaxed as she took a license plate out of her backpack.

"The first thing any police officer will do if they're

looking for a car like mine is run the license plates. These will come up clean."

"Why do you even have those?"

She gnawed on the side of her lip. "Actually, six months ago I had five different clean license plates, to use if I had to run from the Organization. I got rid of all but one."

He scrubbed a hand across his face. "Well, I'm glad you only have one illegal set."

"In the interest of full disclosure, I also have a credit card and ID under another name." She flinched at his thunderous look. "I—I…I'm trying, Tanner, I promise. But running and disappearing was my whole life for so long."

She didn't want him to be disappointed in her, and she'd tried to force herself to get rid of the bag multiple times, but she just couldn't.

His face relaxed, and his hand reached for hers. "I know. And who am I to judge, considering you're using all this stuff to help me? But let's try to keep the illegal activities as much to a minimum as possible. And when we get all this cleared up, how about getting rid of all the illegal stuff."

She nodded. Maybe by then the thought wouldn't send her into a panic.

He took the license plate from her and changed it out. Then they got back on the road.

"We need to come up with a plan," she said after a few more minutes. "Driving around puts us at unnecessary risk. I know you don't want me to use the fake ID or credit card, but that will allow us to get a hotel room. All we need is somewhere with good internet and I can start to look into the situation."

Which would involve more illegal activity, but she didn't want to bring that up.

But she wasn't fooling him. His lips tightened. "What systems are you going to hack?"

She sighed. "I was going to start with the sheriff's office. I should be able to find all the details of the latest murder there. Then cross-reference them with Darin Carrico and see if there's an association. I also want to see if he sent out another email before Owen Duquette was killed."

Tanner nodded, not giving her a hard time about the hacking she would need to do. At this point, there was no way around it. They needed info and they needed it fast. The best she could do was promise to only access the info they needed.

She was capable of so much more.

"Will Grand County be able to trace where the hack is coming from? Find you?"

Bree actually laughed out loud at the absurdity of that statement.

A half smile lit his face. "I guess that's a no."

"Believe me, there's very few people outside of the ones from the Organization we put in prison a few months ago who would be able to do a back trace on me."

"Okay, because if we've got to bend some laws, I want to make sure none of it comes back on you."

"Believe me, it won't."

"Then I've got the perfect place for us to go. We'll actually have to circle back toward Risk Peak, but it's far enough away that we won't run into anyone. A cabin, but with security and Wi-Fi. I'll have to make a call first to some of Noah's former Special Forces teammates."

She nodded. "Okay, we can get a burner phone when we stop for gas. Any truck rest stop off the interstate will have them."

A few minutes later, they were pulling up to a gas station. Bree grabbed two baseball caps from her bag.

She handed one to him. "Stay in the car and keep this as low over your eyes as possible. Don't look around, just look down at your hands like you're messing with a phone. I'll get the gas."

She could tell right away he didn't like that. "No."

She rolled her eyes. "I'm much less conspicuous than you are, Tanner. I've got more experience blending in, plus I'm not half a foot taller than everybody else around me."

His lips pressed together in a mutinous line, but he finally gave her a brief nod.

Bree got out of the car, pumping the gas then going inside to pay and find a burner phone. She kept her head down and eyes averted—not a problem for her.

She was going to have to work quickly once Tanner got them to the cabin. He said he'd give it three days, but she was betting after two he'd be ready to turn himself in.

Tanner Dempsey was never going to be good at hiding. It went against his nature. Even when he had worked undercover, she was sure they hadn't used him as someone who blended in.

But she would find out what was going on. Because there was no way she was letting him go to jail.

Chapter Seventeen

"We're going to need to break into the sheriff's office."

Tanner's head flew up at Bree's words. It was after 2:00 a.m., and she'd been working nonstop for the last twelve hours, digging up whatever she could about the three murders.

If he had thought he felt helpless when he was just supposed to keep out of the way of the investigation, it was nothing compared to how he felt knowing someone was out there actively trying to frame him.

That was where they'd started in their research: Who held some sort of grudge against Tanner?

Ended up that was a pretty long list when they'd included everyone he'd arrested or stopped from completing some sort of nefarious plan.

"Break into the sheriff's office?" he asked. "Adding to the list of crimes I'm wanted for doesn't seem like the best of plans," he responded, walking over and rubbing her shoulders. She leaned her head back against his stomach. "Is it some sort of information you can't get to electronically?"

"Evidently, Sheriff Duggan has pretty important info that she's not entering into her normal computer system. Is that strange?"

He nodded. "She's got a separate computer in her office, without any sort of internet connection to it at all. She calls it her diary."

Bree's eyes narrowed, but she obviously had respect for Sheriff Duggan's tactics. "Smart."

"Definitely. Not to mention she knows what you're capable of. She knows that any information stored in a computer connected to the internet can be accessed by you if you put your mind to it."

Bree reached back and grabbed his waist with her hands, tilting her head back so she was looking at him, upside down. "I only found out about it because she mentioned it in an e-memo to her assistant. Do you think Sheriff Duggan thinks you're guilty now?"

"I hope not. But me not being there to explain myself is certainly not helping."

He knew word had gotten around Risk Peak that there was a warrant out for his arrest. He couldn't even think too much about how that made the people who knew him feel. They trusted him to uphold the law. To now be on the opposite side of the law was almost unfathomable.

"I should turn myself in. I might have to sit in a cell for a couple of weeks, but we'll get this cleared up."

Bree stood and turned so she was facing him, climbing up onto the chair on her knees. "I support you. I really do. But let's see what's in the sheriff's office. If it's nothing important then, heck, you'll already be in the building, and you can turn yourself in then if you want."

Bree was still working the Carrico angle—had been all day—but she hadn't come up with anything to tie him to this third victim. He and Duquette had never served any prison time together or seemed to have any ties any other way. Bree hadn't found any email sent by Carrico concerning Duquette.

She'd spent more time looking at the first two emails concerning Newkirk and Anders, convinced something wasn't right, frustrated when she couldn't figure out what it was.

She pulled back to return to her computer, but he grasped her hips and kept her in place in front of him. "Okay, we go to the sheriff's office and see if there's anything that throws major light on the case. In for a penny, in for a pound, right?"

As far as Bree had told him from the "watchful eye" she was keeping on the sheriff's office in Risk Peak, they believed that he was making the most of his administrative leave and had gone on that romantic getaway. For once, small-town rumor was working in his favor.

But if they figured out that wasn't the case, it would become a manhunt. So figuring out what the sheriff was keeping on her private computer was probably a good idea, even if the thought of it was distasteful.

An hour later they were going through a basement side door into the Grand County Sheriff's Department office. It should've had a fire alarm on it, but Tanner knew some of the guys had disconnected it because it provided an easy way in and out for a smoke break.

He grimaced as the door made a loud creak as they opened it. If they got caught, it wasn't technically illegal to be using that door, but it sure as hell was going to raise a lot of questions.

Fortunately, there wasn't anything happening in these administrative offices in the back of the building at this time of night. There was more life on the south side of the building—a holding cell and the night officers' offices. But they shouldn't need to go there for any reason.

He kept a hand at Bree's back as he led her down the darkened hall toward Sheriff Duggan's office. She had her laptop gripped tightly in her arms. She hadn't offered a reason why she'd brought it, and he hadn't asked.

Sheriff Duggan's office door wasn't locked, which only made him feel marginally better about opening it and ushering Bree inside. At least so far he hadn't actually had to break in. But he was committed now. If there was fallout, he'd have to deal with it. He wasn't going to second-guess himself any more.

Bree immediately moved over to a laptop sitting at the corner of Duggan's desk. "This is it."

"Work as fast as you can."

Bree was pretty damn fast.

She had the sheriff's computer opened and had hacked her way past the password in under two minutes. "Got it."

He whistled through his teeth. "You're scary fast there, freckles. Passwords don't seem to give you any trouble."

She smiled. "Passwords are nothing more than a security blanket for the general public. They definitely don't keep any true hackers from getting what they want."

He shook his head. "Promise me you'll always stay on my side of the law."

Of course, which side was his right at this moment? Tanner didn't examine that too closely.

"Okay, Sheriff Duggan," Bree whispered to the computer. "Tell dear diary what's on your mind."

A few minutes later, Bree reached a hand out toward him without looking back at him. "Oh my gosh, come look at this."

"Is it bad?"

She shook her head. "No, it's definitely not bad. She's kept a record of dozens of phone calls, messages and meetings she's had today. All about you."

"What?" He rushed to her side.

She showed him what she was talking about on the screen. Sure enough, at least a dozen people, from Risk Peak and other parts of Grand County, had contacted the sheriff basically as character witnesses on his behalf. Obviously some of them didn't have all their facts straight—gossip was fast in a town Risk Peak's size, but rarely accurate—but they'd all rushed to his defense when they'd heard about the arrest warrant.

"She's keeping a very meticulous list of everyone defending you," Bree said. "Some of these are pretty impressive character witnesses."

He was honored and more than ever wanted to clear this up so he could get back to serving the town he loved so much.

Bree started clicking away on the computer again. "Okay, let's see what else is going on inside the sheriff's mind. Because as touching as that is, it's not going to help clear your name."

Tanner resumed his lookout through the cracked door as Bree went back to work. It didn't take long for her to find the other info.

"There you are," she whispered. "The sheriff doesn't want to say it publicly, but she has some concerns about someone in the office. She discovered someone else who was a connection between all three victims."

"Who?"

"Hang on." She clicked a few keys, then paused. "Dr. Craig Michalski."

Shock ricocheted through his body. "What?"

"He was the official county psychiatrist for both Newkirk and Anders. Was even asked to come in for a second opinion for Anders for the parole board.

That was one of the reasons Anders was released—because Michalski suggested it."

Tanner rubbed his eyes. He had known Michalski had visited Carrico, although still didn't know why. The fact that he'd been the psychiatrist assigned to Newkirk and Anders wasn't really surprising. Dr. Michalski was part of a lot of cases. "Okay. Keep going."

"Says here that the sheriff approved the doc's request to talk to Duquette about eleven months ago while Duquette was in prison." She looked up from the computer and met his eyes. "Because Michalski was trying to understand more about you."

Tanner scrubbed a hand over his face. A year ago he'd hit a particular rough spot with his PTSD. He'd been angry, for sure, frustrated at his inability to just move past everything. Had been frustrated at the lack of noticeable progress in his therapy.

"Dr. Michalski and I haven't always seen eye to eye. But I'm going to be the first one to argue that just because you happen to know three people doesn't mean you killed them."

She nodded. "Granted. But Sheriff Duggan has some concerns. She's afraid Dr. Michalski has some sort of personal problem with you. She also says he's been acting erratically over the past three months. Enough for her to have real uneasiness."

"Damn it," he muttered.

"That's basically all that's on this computer." She closed it. "Tanner, I know you don't want to jump to conclusions, but Michalski would've known how to taint a crime scene with your DNA. He told the sheriff and Ryan Fletcher that he thought you were actively capable of committing murder. What if he has some sort of vendetta against you or something?"

Had that been true and Tanner had just missed it? There was definitely no love lost between him and Dr. Michalski, but would the man murder people in order to frame Tanner?

A light flipping on in the far hallway caught his attention.

"We've got to go, now," he said, holding out his hand for Bree.

She closed the computers, and when he heard footsteps in the direction they needed to go, he rushed her out the door and down the opposite direction they'd come in. It would force them to circle back, but at least they'd be able to do that undetected.

Tanner picked up speed and rounded the corner, Bree's hand in his.

And ran straight into Dr. Michalski.

"What the hell?" Tanner let go of Bree, placing himself between her and the doctor. "What are you doing here, Michalski?"

This was one of the most isolated sections of the building. There wasn't much reason for Dr. Michalski to be down here at all, and especially not in the middle of the night.

The doctor shifted back and forth, more agitated than Tanner had ever seen him.

"What am *I* doing here? What are you doing here, Tanner? Do you know there's a warrant out for your arrest?"

Tanner grabbed the man by his shirt and pressed him up against the wall. "Actually, yes, I do know that. And part of the reason for said warrant is because of your statement to the sheriff that you thought I was capable of murdering those guys."

"I did nothing more than offer my honest opinion of whether you had the mental and emotional capacity for the act. Whether you want to admit it or not, you are capable of it."

Tanner didn't disagree, but that wasn't the point. He didn't let go of the other man's shirt.

"But in the context of when and why it was being asked, you just threw me under the bus, Doc. Knowing there was a connection between me and all three victims and how it would look."

Michalski shifted nervously again. His eyes darted all over the place before finally settling back on Tanner. "I was just offering my professional opinion. Valuable information."

"Really? Then why didn't you offer other valuable information, too? Like the fact that *you* had contact with all three victims."

The doctor cleared his throat. "My job brought me in contact with all three of them."

"So did mine." Tanner had to force himself to keep his voice down. "I didn't do this. I didn't kill those men, as much as circumstantial evidence and your opinion of my psyche might suggest otherwise."

"If you're not guilty, just turn yourself in. All this will get sorted out."

"Speaking of guilt." Bree peeked out from around Tanner before he could stop her. "Why are you here at three o'clock in the morning?"

"Especially in this part of the building?" Tanner added. "There's no reason for you to be back here at all if you're not up to something."

The other man's eyes bolted around nervously again. "No offense, but I'm not the one who has a warrant out for my arrest. I don't have to give a reason for being here."

Tanner was about to argue the point none too gently with the doctor when a ping came from Bree's laptop behind him. A second later she grabbed his arm.

"Whitaker just logged in to a computer on site. We need to go."

What the hell was Whitaker doing here at three o'clock in the morning? He didn't work night shifts, either.

"Tanner," Michalski said, his voice returning to the soothing tone he was more familiar with. "Just turn yourself in right now. There's been a ton of people who've come in or called to speak up on your behalf. If you didn't do this, trust your colleagues to find the real killer."

"Yeah, Doc? Well, you're a colleague and you

certainly didn't speak up on my behalf. So I think it might be to my benefit to prove my own innocence."

Tanner dragged the older man down the hallway and threw him into a closet, bolting the door from the outside. Michalski would be able to get someone's attention tomorrow when the administrative offices filled up.

He looked over at Bree. "You okay?"

She nodded. "Yeah, but let's get out of here. The turning-yourself-in plan doesn't seem like such a good one anymore."

A door clicked open at the other end of the hallway. Tanner grabbed Bree's hand, and they ran in the opposite direction, barely making it around the corner without being seen.

Tanner didn't slow down. If Michalski made enough noise, whoever was around would undoubtedly hear him. And if it was Whitaker—although why would Whitaker have a reason to be in that part of the office at that time of night, either?—the chase might be starting immediately.

They needed to get out of the building right now. But the only way to do that was going back the way they'd come.

"We're trapped, aren't we?" she whispered.

He let out a low curse. "Whoever that is, it won't take them long to get to the closet I stuffed Michalski in."

She nodded and dropped to the floor, opening her computer and resting it on her crossed legs. Within just a few seconds, an alarm was going off at the front of the building.

"What is that?" he asked her.

She shrugged, getting up. "I triggered a window alarm near the northeast side corner of the building. It won't buy us much time—"

He pulled her in for a quick, hard kiss. "But it will be enough."

They were getting out of here and figuring out exactly what the hell was going on.

Chapter Eighteen

The man looked at report after report after report that had been shown to him. Reports of how Tanner Dempsey could not be guilty.

He was their hero.

He was incapable of wrong.

How could the people here be so blind? Dempsey had managed to completely pull the wool over everyone's eyes. Convinced them he was infallible.

He was so, so fallible.

The people in this town, this county, obviously couldn't see what was right in front of them. Their letters proved how much Dempsey had fooled them. They argued for his innocence out of hand, never suspecting that Dempsey was the epitome of everything wrong with law enforcement.

Tanner Dempsey wasn't a hero; he was a villain. He should be shunned, not cheered. If it were anyone else who was accused of three murders, there'd be a statewide manhunt, rather than everyone sitting around twiddling their thumbs, waiting for Dempsey to come back from his *romantic getaway* and explain himself.

As if he could explain away the darkness that encompassed his very soul.

The man realized he had miscalculated. Dempsey was never going to be taken down this way. Never going to rot in prison like the man had envisioned. There were too many people who would insist on his innocence even if he walked up and stabbed them in the chest.

Dempsey was certainly capable of it; the man knew that without a doubt.

The thought that Dempsey wouldn't pay for his crimes was unbearable.

But every day that he was allowed to run free, he came closer to clearing his name.

Because of that woman. The one who looked at him with such devotion in her eyes.

First, Dempsey fooled everyone into believing that he was an upstanding man of the law. And now he would also get to fall in love? To have a life and a happy ending with a beautiful woman? To not pay for his sins in any way?

It was time for a game change. Life in prison was too good for Dempsey.

Instead, Dempsey would lose *everything*. Starting with the woman and ending with his life.

Chapter Nineteen

They hadn't even made it back to Bree's car and gotten back on the highway toward the cabin before she had her laptop open and was researching Dr. Craig Michalski. He was the key to all this.

She used a mobile hot spot from the burner to gather data on the drive, frustrated when it couldn't provide her information fast enough. When they pulled up to the cabin, she went inside without a word, still carrying the laptop with one hand and typing with the other.

Tanner was smart enough to just stay out of her way.

"Sheriff Duggan is right to be worried about Michalski. About four months ago, his behavior and financial patterns changed. He started spending a lot more money and spending a lot more time away from home."

Tanner was pacing behind her at the cabin. "That's not necessarily a sign of guilt. Could be a midlife crisis or something equally benign."

That was true. "But it also could be an indication that he was mentally or emotionally snapping."

Tanner's hands rested on her shoulders. "Do me a favor. Come at this as if you're trying to prove Dr. Michalski is innocent rather than prove he's guilty."

"Why?"

He kissed the top of her head. "Because that's what I would want someone to do for me. Plus, it might provide you a new way to look at things. Not to mention, if Michalski wanted to frame me, he could've done it long before now."

Bree actually wanted to growl, but refrained. How the heck did he expect her to prove *him* innocent if she was trying to prove everyone else innocent, too?

"Best I can do is neutral," she muttered. "Definitely not treating him like I think he's innocent."

"Fair enough."

"Assuming that Michalski's behavioral changes have nothing to do with the three dead bodies he had contact with and failed to mention…then what really doesn't fall in line is Carrico."

Tanner resumed his pacing behind her, but she kept her eyes on her computer. "You're right," he said. "Michalski had legitimate reason to be around all three victims, but we don't know why he was talking to Carrico."

She pulled back up the encoded emails Carrico had sent. "Do you think they could be working together? That Michalski is on the other end of that guerrilla email account?"

"Is there any indication that Michalski and Carrico know each other?"

Bree split her computer screen so she could see the prison guest log on one section and Michalski's phone record on the other. She wrote a tiny program very quickly to search through both for the commonalities they were looking for.

It didn't take long for the results. "Nothing obvious. If Michalski called him, it wasn't with his cell, office or home phone. Three days ago was the only time he's ever visited Carrico. No obvious phone calls or emails from Colorado Correctional."

He shook his head. "I've got to believe that if the two of them were working together, Dr. Michalski would be too smart to go visit Carrico so overtly like that. Especially right in the middle of all this going down."

She shrugged. "Or maybe it never occurred to him that we'd make the connection. It was pretty thin. But…"

"But what?" he asked, standing behind her again.

"There's something not right about these emails Carrico sent. The ones with the cipher codes." She couldn't quite put her finger on it, but she knew she was missing something.

"Are you sure you cracked them correctly?"

"Definitely. I just feel like I didn't look at the source code thoroughly enough. I took the messages at face value, because it was showing me what I wanted to see—that you were innocent." She tapped her temple. "I should know better."

She had all this skill when it came to computers, but when it mattered most she couldn't seem to figure out whatever it was she was missing.

Why was Dr. Michalski talking to Carrico? The others were legitimate connections, but there was no reason he should've been talking to Carrico.

And these emails from Carrico to whoever was on the other end of that burner email. Something was off about those, too. Carrico didn't strike her as someone who would use a cipher to communicate. The delicate nature of the code just didn't seem to be his style.

"It's time for me to turn myself in," Tanner said. Except for bouncing information off the other, he hadn't spoken much since they got back to the cabin. He'd stood looking out the window. She'd known it was just a matter of time before those words would come out of his mouth.

"They know I'm running now," he continued. "Michalski, guilty or not, will sing like a canary. So they'll up the search. They're going to put pressure on my family, call Noah in for questioning. I can't let the people I care about pay the price." He walked over and kissed the top of her head. "I can't let *you* pay the price. If we go back in now, there shouldn't be many repercussions for you."

She sighed. If that was what he wanted to do, she would support him. But if he would just give them a little more time…and do something she knew he was going to fight.

She stood and wrapped her arms around his waist. "I know I might sound like a broken record, but before you turn yourself in, there's one more thing I want us to try."

"What?"

"Let's go visit Carrico again. He's the key to cracking this open. There's too much about his situation—the emails, his ties to two of the victims, but not three—that's illogical. But most important, why was Michalski there talking to him just three days ago?"

Tanner let out a harsh breath. "I can't go inside the prison. My ID will ping law enforcement immediately and let them know I'm there. Plus, Carrico hates cops anyway. He's not going to talk to me."

She backed away a little bit and pointed to her chest. "But he might talk to me. I'll go. Maybe I can figure out whatever it was we missed the first time."

Tanner backed away, crossing his arms over his chest and leaning back against the wall. She'd known he wasn't going to like the idea.

"No," he said. "And before you ask, it's not because I don't think you can do it, but because it's not worth the risk. Your name is probably tagged in the system, too. As soon as you show them your ID, it's going to tip off the same people as if I had done it."

If he hadn't liked the first part of the plan, he definitely wasn't going to like the second. "Or… I can use the ID I had in my bug-out bag. It's never been utilized—it's completely clean. It definitely won't raise any red flags."

Tanner didn't move from where he was standing. Those brown eyes of his were shuttered. "Still no. Carrico could be a killer. Sending you back in there does nothing but put you on his radar. Three men are already dead. I don't want to put you at risk, too."

She walked over until she was standing right in front of him and raised her hands until they were caressing the outside of his biceps under his Henley shirt.

"I don't think Darin is the killer. All this played out just a little too nicely, don't you think?"

"He's our most likely suspect and we can't ignore that. Just because he might have gotten someone else to do it rather than pull the trigger himself wouldn't make him any less of a killer. I feel for him in his situation with his daughter, but that doesn't mean I can deny the evidence we found."

"But that evidence has holes. Like it's leading us somewhere that's definitely going to be a dead end." She squeezed his arms. "If you could get in there to talk to him without letting law enforcement know where you are, would you think it was worth it to talk to Carrico one more time?"

She could almost see his teeth grinding in his jaw. "Maybe."

"What does your gut say about Carrico?"

Tanner let out a sigh. "Fine. You're right, okay?

Right up until the point where you found those encoded emails, I was completely buying into his story. But somebody framing him and me? We're really getting into conspiracy-theories territory here."

"Tanner, just let me talk to him and find out what Dr. Michalski said. I'll do it today while he's still at Colorado Correctional and we can still get in contact with him. If he's really about to get moved up to the max-security prison, it will be harder to get info from him there."

She could see him struggling with the idea.

"Team, remember?" she said. "I'm not arguing with you about turning yourself in. I know you think that's the right thing to do, and I support that. But let's do it with as much information as possible."

His arms came around her and jerked her to his chest. "I don't like it, but I can't deny what you're saying."

Thank God.

"Let's start some coffee. We've got a few hours left before visiting starts. Let me see what else I can find out about Michalski."

Tanner kissed the top of her head and pushed her toward the laptop, then went to make both coffee and breakfast for them. Bree didn't waste any time. She immediately hacked back into the Grand County Sheriff's Department system. She quickly wrote a program to send her a message anytime Tanner's name was used by anyone in any department.

It didn't take long to figure out they definitely

knew Tanner was evading them now. There was a full search going on for him.

She winced as a new alert came across her screen.

"What?" he asked as he refilled her empty coffee cup.

"You were right. Whitaker brought Noah in for questioning."

Tanner gave a brief nod. "Not surprising. We share a residence, and everyone in town knows how close we are."

She knew how much Noah loved the outdoors, how much he hated people. "Will he be all right?"

"Noah can handle himself. He'll keep it together however long he needs to. It helps that he doesn't know a damn thing about what's going on, not that he would hesitate to lie to help me." Tanner's tone was light, but there was a heaviness to his stance now.

She reached up and cupped his cheek. "I'll work faster."

He gave her another tight nod then turned back toward the kitchen.

Bree dug deeper into every file she could find. She had to be more careful; the sheriff's department had obviously brought in some sort of computer specialist to try to track her.

It almost provided a challenge.

In the end it was Tanner's advice to treat Michalski as if he *wasn't* guilty that led her in the direction she needed to go. And it definitely hadn't been what she'd been expecting.

"Tanner, look at this."

She turned the screen so he could see it more easily and brought up a backdoor list of all Dr. Michalski's patient files. Including Tanner's.

Tanner began to read.

"What exactly am I looking for here? Something specific?"

"This is a relatively sophisticated back channel into Michalski's files. I should have needed to build this grouping one file at a time, but I didn't."

"What does that mean?"

"It means someone has already hacked Dr. Michalski's files. It's impossible for me to tell who from here. I'd need access to his computer. All I can tell you is that it was a reasonably well-done job."

Tanner rubbed his fingers over his eyes. "This case just keeps getting stranger and stranger. Like there's some puppet master pulling the strings that we can't see."

She couldn't have agreed more. "Then we start yanking on strings of our own and see what happens. And I think we should start with Carrico."

Chapter Twenty

Kelsey Collins entered the Colorado Correctional visitors' area right when it opened that afternoon. Bree wasn't surprised when none of the guards who had checked her in a few days ago recognized her. Her brown hair was tucked up under a short blond wig. Her freckles were covered by a pound of makeup. Her whole posture was different than how she normally carried herself.

And they all matched the ID she'd handed the guard as she checked in. The guard had scanned it and handed it back to her when it came back clean.

Bree had not doubted it would.

Tanner, on the other hand, was a half step above a nervous wreck waiting out in the car. For a few minutes—especially when she'd come out of the bathroom in full Kelsey Collins gear—she hadn't thought he was going to let her do this. Could almost see him trying to find a way that he could take the risk on himself rather than allow her to do it.

The fact that he *really* didn't want her doing this

had actually made her desire to do it even greater. She could practically feel Tanner's concern and need to protect her surrounding her like a cocoon.

It was…nice.

So much more than nice. It was what she'd been waiting for her whole life and never thought she'd find.

Damn it, she wanted to help clear Tanner's name so they could go on that getaway he'd talked about. Whoever this master puppeteer was, he needed to be stopped, not only because of all the bad murderer stuff but because he was getting in the way of Bree's love life.

She'd never had one before, and now that she did, she was tired of waiting.

Bree kept her Kelsey Collins persona wrapped around her as she walked to an empty visitors' table, just a couple down from where they'd met with Carrico last time. She refused to let her fears—not that she would get hurt, but that she wasn't capable of doing this—get the best of her. She would talk to Carrico, study every bit of his nonverbal behavior that she could and get the answers she needed.

The Kelsey Collins disguise didn't fool Carrico very long. He hadn't been across from Bree more than a few seconds before his eyes narrowed.

"You're looking a bit different than the last time I saw you, cop lady friend, not that I mind the blond. Where's Mr. Cop today? You decide to trade up for a real man?"

Carrico was slouched in his chair, face set in a half smirk. Bree forced herself to look deeper at the man, beyond the surface conceit and attitude. To study him the way Tanner would if he was here.

Carrico's thin face was even more gaunt than it had been a few days ago. Dark circles had taken up residence under his eyes. The man was worried. Not nearly as flippant as he pretended to be.

She needed to get through to him and keep him from becoming defensive. Otherwise he'd never talk to her. She didn't have any sort of interrogation training. She barely had any sort of *conversation* training.

She decided to go with what she did have: the truth.

"I owe you some thanks. Because of you I figured out I was in love with Tanner."

One of his eyebrows shot up almost comically. "And how is that, exactly?"

"Because after we left here three days ago, Tanner planned to help you with your situation regardless of whether you'd given him any useful information to help him out or not."

Carrico shrugged, not looking impressed.

"Tanner has his own problems," she continued. "Believe it or not, ones just as big as yours, but he still planned to help you—even though he doesn't know you and you acted like a complete jackass when we talked last. He wants to help you because that's just the type of person Tanner is. Someone who does the right thing, even when it doesn't benefit him personally."

He'd done that with her, too. Risked everything to protect her and get her out of a situation where she would've died.

Tanner Dempsey was courageous, strong, smart and just a little bit broken. Bree didn't know a lot about feelings, but she knew with absolute clarity that she was in love with him.

"Yeah, well, I'm still going to Colorado State Penitentiary, so I'm not feeling like your boy is such a golden angel."

She leaned forward. "He has to get himself out of trouble before he can help you. But he will help you, Darin."

"My brother says not to trust cops. Not to talk to anyone else."

"Believe me, I know what it's like to trust no one but yourself. But I promise you, if Tanner can get himself clear of his own charges, he will do what he can to help you. Don't you want to be able to know you did everything you could to be able to see your daughter?"

He didn't say anything, but she felt like she was getting through to him. "I can tell you're not sleeping well—I know that feeling, too. Staying awake, trying to figure out if you missed anything. If anything can be done to change the situation you're in. I know what it's like to sit alone with my own desperation, Darin. Tanner will help you. He's a man of his word. I've bet my whole life on it."

He let out a sigh and leaned in toward the table. "Fine. What do you want to know?"

"Why was Dr. Michalski here last week?"

Darin shrugged. "He was my last resort. I knew he'd talked to both Anders and Newkirk, and that he was part of the reason they'd gotten paroled early. I never could get Dr. Michalski to come talk to me, though, to see if there was anything that could be done about my transfer. Finally, my brother Glen convinced him."

"Do you know how Glen convinced him?"

"Not really. Maybe used the cancer card." His face tightened in grief. "Glen has Stage IV lung cancer. So maybe he played on the doc's sympathy."

Stage IV cancer. That would explain why Glen had looked even more gaunt than Darin when she'd seen him.

"Did Dr. Michalski say anything about Tanner when he was here?"

Carrico rolled his eyes. "Are you kidding? No. The guy would barely even talk about my situation. All he wanted to know was about how Glen knew his wife. How the hell am I supposed to know that? All I know is about what's in here. Glen has his own life."

This was it. The piece they'd been missing. "Glen knows Dr. Michalski's wife? How?"

He snorted. "I can't really keep track of my brother's whereabouts from in here. But whatever. I think they both work in the courthouse together or something. Both of them do IT computer stuff."

Which meant Glen could definitely have been the one to hack Dr. Michalski's files.

"Do you think Glen tried to blackmail Michalski into coming to talk to you?"

The rest of Darin's tough-guy facade fell away. "Glen has taken care of me since we were kids. He hates that I'm in here. He was helping my ex take care of Sharon, my daughter, sending them money and stuff. Keeping an eye on Sharon and making sure my ex treats her right."

"He sounds like a good guy."

"He's the best. But now with the cancer, he's…" Darin trailed off, shrugging, obviously unable to say the word *dying*. "I don't know what I'm going to do without him. Especially once they send me to max security, he won't be able to visit because he's so sick. He didn't say that, but I could tell. And he's only got a couple months left anyway."

It wasn't difficult to see Glen was pretty damn sick. "So he got Dr. Michalski here to talk to you to see if he would recommend an earlier release for you like he had Newkirk and Anders."

Darin nodded. "I wasn't even hoping for early release, just maybe to see if he could get me kept here."

"Did Dr. Michalski mention an Owen Duquette when you talked to him? Or do you know him?"

There was no light of recognition in Darin's eyes. "No. Who is he?"

She shook her head. "Nobody important. So you don't know how Glen finally got Dr. Michalski here to visit?"

"Nope. All I know is that the good doctor sure as hell wasn't interested in helping me with my situation."

Bree had been wrong. It was *Glen* Carrico they needed to talk to, not Darin. But there was still one thing that didn't make sense—those emails she'd discovered with the cipher. The more she talked to Darin, the less sense it made.

She decided to come at it from a side angle rather than directly. "How old is Sharon again? Do you get to talk to her a lot right now? Phone? Email?"

Darin rubbed his hand across his face. "She's four. We talk a little on the phone—twice a week. No email, but that's probably more me than her."

"You guys don't get email in here?"

"No, we do, but computers are Glen's jive, not mine. I haven't touched one since I've been in here."

She stared at him. Was he lying? She didn't think so but couldn't be sure. What he was saying made more sense than the complexly coded emails that seemed to have come from him. "Never? You've never emailed any friends or former associates? Your brother?"

Darin shook his head. "Nah. They know to call me if they want to talk. I can't type worth a damn."

It was time to ask him straight up. "So you never sent anyone a message about Anders or Newkirk?"

"Why does everybody care about them so much? I barely knew the guys when they were here, much less now. I can't even remember what Anders looks like."

"Everybody cares because they're both dead. Murdered." She hoped she wasn't making a big mistake by telling him this.

Darin's eyes got wide before he sank back hard against his chair. "They are?" Panic fell over his features. "Wait—do the cops think I had something to do with it?"

She shook her head. "Actually, the cops suspect Tanner did it."

He relaxed a little. "Oh. Your man does have some pretty big problems, then. Why are you asking me about them?"

Bree believed Darin was legitimately surprised at the news of their deaths. "You're the only other person who seemed to know them both, besides Dr. Michalski and Tanner. I was hoping you could remember talking to anyone about them."

"No, only to Glen when we were trying to figure out a way to keep me here, rather than going up to state pen. I just remembered that Anders and Newkirk had both made deals that had gotten them out early."

Glen again. Time was running out, and they needed to talk to him.

"That other guy you mentioned. Duquette. He dead, too?"

There didn't seem much point in lying. "Yes. Unfortunately."

He whistled through his teeth. "Then no offense, but glad I don't know him."

Even though it went against her nature, she reached over and touched Darin's hand. "I've got to go. But I promise Tanner will look into what's going on with your transfer."

"Sounds like your man has trouble enough of his own to worry about."

She nodded and let go of his hand. "He does. But I'm going to make sure that gets cleared up. And once I do, he won't forget about you."

He just gave a one-shoulder shrug. "I won't hold my breath. I've been forgotten by damn near everyone."

Before she could say anything further, he stood and walked toward the door.

THE HOUR BREE was inside the prison was one of the longest of Tanner's life. He alternated between cursing himself for allowing her to do this at all and remembering that she was a genius and had handled circumstances worse than this since she was twelve years old.

Still, seeing her walking toward him with her unnaturally blond hair meant he could finally let out the breath he'd been holding for the past hour. Her gait was leisurely, and she was pretending to talk on the telephone—both smart. Nothing about her drew any sort of attention. She could be one of any hundreds of women her age walking across a parking lot.

He forced himself to stay in the car. It was the least he could do in order to help her sell her act.

But it took every ounce of his control not to grab her and pull her into his arms and never let her out again.

"Any problems?" he asked when she got in beside him.

"We have all sorts of problems, but if you're asking if I had any trouble getting inside, then no."

Thank God. Tanner started the car and pulled out of the parking lot. "Okay, so what were the problems?"

She began taking out the pins that held her wig in place. "This is probably going to sound like I'm just trying not to start my sexual experience as part of a conjugal visit with you…but you can't turn yourself in yet."

He swallowed a bark of laughter. This woman. "Colorado doesn't allow conjugal visits, but I'll still hear you out on why I can't turn myself in yet."

"I think this is all more complicated than we even thought."

He didn't even try to stop himself from rolling his eyes. "Of course it is. What did you find out?"

"I don't think Darin Carrico had anything to do with the murders. I told him Anders and Newkirk were dead, and he legitimately seemed surprised."

"What about the emails he sent?"

"I don't think he sent them at all. Someone just made it look like he did. If I look a little deeper, I wouldn't be surprised if I found the emails hadn't originated from Camp George West at all. Damn it, I should've looked into that further rather than take it at face value. It was stupid."

He reached over and placed his hand on hers, which had curled up into fists on her lap. One of his hands could cover both of hers. "Hey. You're doing the best you can under much less than optimal circumstances. If it wasn't for you, I'd be sitting in a cell with zero information about what was going on."

"It was still a careless mistake."

"Yeah, well, your mistakes are still providing us forward progress, so let's focus on that. If you don't think Carrico has anything to do with the murders, then who do you think is involved?"

"I think all the answers might be with *Glen* Carrico, not Darin. Evidently he somehow knows Michalski's wife, and I think Glen might be the one who hacked the doctor's files."

"And he's setting up his brother to look like the murderer? They seemed pretty friendly a few days ago."

"No, I don't think so. I'll have to dig deeper about the emails. But I definitely think Glen is the puzzle piece we've been missing in all this."

He squeezed her hands. "Then you're right. It's time to pay the other Carrico brother a visit."

Chapter Twenty-One

Glen Carrico's house was far away from damn near everything. The longer they drove down his isolated drive, the more uncomfortable Tanner became.

"What do we know about this guy again?"

Bree had held her computer in her lap since they'd pulled away from the prison almost an hour ago.

"Glen Carrico. Older brother of Darin. Thirty-two years old, never married. No known significant other. Has lived at this address pretty much all of his adult life."

"And he and his brother are close?"

Bree side-eyed him. "Juvenile records are a bit trickier to…access, but from what I've seen, yeah, they are definitely close. Looks like Glen took on responsibility for raising Darin when their mom took off. Glen was eighteen years old at the time. Darin was eleven. Glen pretty much gave up a lot of his future to take care of his brother."

Tanner grimaced. "Glen got any sort of record himself?"

Bree shook her head. "Nothing. Honestly, it looks like he was a good kid. Got accepted to Colorado State with a full scholarship, but declined. Did his best trying to raise his troubled brother."

"He couldn't have been very happy that Darin ended up in jail."

"Definitely not, and even more upset when they gave notice two months ago that they're transferring him to max security. He's written memos to just about every person with a pulse in the Colorado law enforcement system, trying to get Darin's situation changed."

Tanner grimaced. "I'll be honest—I don't really understand what Glen has to do with any of this. He doesn't have any ties with the victims and has never been in trouble with the law."

She nodded. "And Glen is dying of cancer. Only has a couple months left to live, according to Darin."

Tanner muttered a curse under his breath. People with nothing left to lose sometimes couldn't be trusted. Added an extra layer of risk he and Bree definitely didn't need.

A small, run-down house finally came into view. Tanner parked in front of it, then reached over and got his Glock from the glove compartment. It didn't look like anyone was home, but Tanner wasn't taking any chances.

"Any possibility I can talk you into staying in the car?" he asked her.

Her sour look answered him before she even got

the words out. "Any chance hell is freezing over in the next thirty seconds?"

He chuckled. "Fine, but be careful."

"Yes, sir, Captain Sexy Lips." She gave him a little salute.

Keeping her close to his side as they approached the front door, Tanner untucked his shirt and placed his weapon in the front waistband of his pants. He didn't like approaching the door without his weapon in hand, but he didn't want Glen mistaking his gun as an act of aggression and responding in kind.

"Glen Carrico, this is Tanner Dempsey. I'm not here in any official capacity. I'd just like to ask you a few questions." Tanner said the words as they approached the broken steps leading up to the door. He listened for a second, but there was no answer.

"Maybe we can talk about Darin and if there's some way I can help him," he called out again.

Still no answer, and as they got closer to the door, Tanner realized it was open just the slightest bit.

He brought his arm out and scooped Bree behind him, pulling his Glock out and pointing it at the ground by his leg.

"Glen?" he called out again.

He dropped his volume. "I really think you ought to consider waiting in the car." He had a very bad feeling about this.

Bree's hands squeezed his waist. "Do you think he's dead?"

"I think it's mighty quiet, and his door is cracked open in the middle of the day. That's not a good sign."

"I'll be okay. I don't want to leave you."

He nodded—he didn't really want her out of his sight, either—and continued forward, weapon raised. He wasn't acting in any sort of law enforcement capacity, but years on the force still had him identifying himself once more at the door. "Glen, I'm coming inside. Your door is open, and I'm worried something is wrong."

Tanner swept Bree over to the side against the house, then nudged the door open with his foot. He gave her a pointed look and mouthed the words *stay here*.

She nodded, and he had to trust she would keep her word. He moved inside, weapon now raised to eye level. He glanced around the room quickly but saw nothing posing danger. Keeping his back to the wall as much as possible, he walked quickly into the small kitchen. Nothing. It didn't take him long to clear the rest of the house.

There wasn't any danger here and, even more important, no dead body.

"It's clear, freckles. You can come in."

"Anything bad?"

He shook his head. "No, thank goodness. I was expecting the worst, and I'm happy not to have found it."

He tucked his gun back into the waistband of his jeans, and the two of them began looking around.

There didn't seem to be anything out of place or any sign of foul play, even with the door cracked open.

Hell, this house was in the middle of nowhere. There was much more chance a wild animal would wander in here than people.

It wasn't till they were near the back of the house and Bree passed by an open window that they heard the music coming from a large shed a couple hundred meters from the back of the house.

"That music wasn't playing when we got out of the car. Maybe Glen is out there," Bree said.

They started the whole process once again. Tanner tried to keep Bree shielded as much as possible as he called out to see if Glen was in the shed and identified himself.

He reached the door and had convinced himself that the man had just left the radio on when a shot fired from over their shoulder and blew out the window at the front of the shed, not five feet from where they were standing.

Bree gave a little scream and Tanner dived for her, knocking them both to the ground, as another shot rang out, this one going a little more wide.

Keeping Bree tucked behind him, Tanner pulled out his gun and fired once in the direction the bullets had come from. There was no way he'd be very accurate from this distance, but it would buy them a second or two.

"Stay low and get inside."

Bree immediately began crawling toward the shed door.

He fired once again, only one time, wanting to save as many bullets as he could in case he needed them, but also wanting to give them a little bit of cover to make it.

Another shot rang out, this one going too high. Bree was inside already, so Tanner dived for the door, yanking it closed behind him.

The shed looked like it hadn't been cleaned out in years. There was stuff everywhere—from stacked tires to old tools to piles of plywood. But the junk worked in their favor.

"Stay low and try to get behind something," he said, guiding her to a spot behind the stack of tires. "If Glen starts shooting blindly the walls won't stop bullets, but the other stuff will."

"Are you sure that's Glen out there? Why's he shooting at us?"

"Maybe he saw me with my gun and got nervous."

Or maybe they'd just found their killer.

"I'll try to give him the benefit of the doubt," he continued. "Mostly because Glen is either a really bad shot or he wasn't trying to hit us. If he had wanted us dead, he could've done it the moment we stepped outside his house, from the angle he was at."

Tanner stepped closer to the door. "This is Captain Tanner Dempsey," he called out. "We just want to talk. Whatever's happening here is a miscommunication."

"I know who you are, cop." That was definitely Glen Carrico's voice.

"I know I had my weapon out, Glen, but that was because your front door was open and I thought there might be danger. It wasn't intended in an aggressive nature toward you. So let's just both put our weapons down and we can talk like reasonable adults."

Glen scoffed. "I don't think I have ever known a cop to be reasonable my whole life. Somehow I don't think today is going to be my lucky day."

"I'm not here as law enforcement, just as a regular person. I just want to talk."

"Tanner Dempsey, hero of Grand County, not here as law enforcement?" Carrico gave a bitter laugh. "I know all about you, Dempsey. And you're not going to get away with what you've been getting away with."

"I don't know what the hell you're talking about, Glen. I didn't kill those guys, so I'm not getting away with anything."

For a long time the other man didn't say anything. When he finally did, Tanner had to strain to hear him.

"You're here earlier than I thought. I thought I had more time."

"More time for what?" Tanner called out when Carrico didn't say anything else. "Glen, come on. Let's talk this out. I'm willing to chalk up the bullets in our direction as a miscommunication. We can still discuss what we're here to talk about."

"What if I don't want to talk to you? Did that ever occur to you, you conceited pig?"

Bree winced from her place crouched behind the tires.

"Fine. Then just let us out. You don't have to talk to us at all. We'll leave."

"No can do, Dempsey." Carrico's contempt was clear the way he spit Tanner's name.

"You can't keep us here. And you don't want to shoot a cop. That will bring all sorts of heat down on you."

"Even if I shoot *you*, Dempsey? My understanding is that you're wanted for murder right now. What if I just say I thought you were trying to attack me and that it was self-defense? After all, you are on my property."

The man did have a valid point.

"I don't think that's really what you want to do, is it, Glen?" Tanner said in the most soothing voice he could muster and still get the volume he needed. "If you'd wanted to kill us, you could've done it already."

Silence followed. Then more silence.

"Do you think he left?" Bree finally asked as the quiet around them dragged out further.

Tanner moved over so he could peek out the window. "Maybe. If he did, we should leave before he changes his mind."

She nodded. "I'm all for that."

Tanner eased the door open. "Glen, we're coming out. Hold your fire. We just want to get to our car and leave."

They both stayed far away from the door as Tanner pushed it open with a stick in case it was a trap. Then held the stick out to see if that would draw fire.

Nothing.

Gritting his teeth, he stuck his hand out long enough for Glen to fire at him, praying he'd be pulling it back with all his fingers still attached.

He did.

It was now or never. He held his hand out to Bree. "Let's go before Glen changes his mind."

Keeping low, they ran out the door. But they weren't two feet away before a shot rang out and the door frame above their heads splintered.

With a low curse, Tanner grabbed Bree around the waist and spun them both back into the shed, slamming the door behind them.

"Yeah, sorry. You leaving isn't going to work out for me after all," Glen yelled.

Chapter Twenty-Two

Tanner's curse was foul. He wasn't sure what had just happened out there, but he knew things had gone from bad to not-going-to-get-out-of-here-alive bad.

"Glen, c'mon, man. Don't do this," he yelled.

"You weren't supposed to come here, Dempsey. Not yet. Damn it, I thought I had more time."

"More time for what?" Tanner yelled. "To help your brother? Do you know who killed Peter Anders and Joshua Newkirk? That's all we want to talk about. We want to figure out what's going on."

"Snitches get stitches, haven't you heard?" Glen sneered.

"Oh my gosh, did he kill them? Is that what he's saying?" Bree's green eyes were big where she crouched behind the tires again.

"I hope not." Not because Tanner wasn't ready to close this case and prove his innocence, but because Glen had the tactical advantage right now with them trapped in the shed. If he was admitting to murder, he definitely wasn't planning on letting them go free to tell the world about it.

"Don't say anything else, Glen," Tanner called out. "Let's just wait and talk things out reasonably."

"I killed them," Glen yelled. "I killed Anders, Newkirk and Owen Duquette."

The words were breathy and quick, like he was relieved to get them off his chest.

Damn it. Tanner ran a hand over his face. He had to get Bree out of this shed. He pulled out his phone. It was time to call in the cavalry.

Proving his innocence wouldn't do him any good if they were both dead.

"Are you calling 911? How long will it take them to get here?" she whispered.

"A while. But I'm not calling them. If they come in here guns blazing, Glen is just going to open fire on this place. I'm calling Whitaker."

She made a sour face. "That guy is an ass hat."

Ass hat or not, Tanner trusted him to have the experience needed for this sort of situation.

Whitaker answered on the first ring. "If it isn't the man on the top of my personal most wanted list."

"Yeah, well, maybe we can go out for dinner and dancing sometime," Tanner quipped. "I need you to get to this address." He rattled it off.

"Glen Carrico's place?"

What the hell? "Do I even want to know why you know that?"

"You're not the only person around here who can

do detective work, you know. I'm actually on my way out to talk to him right now."

Tanner wanted to know exactly how Whitaker had figured it out, but that would have to wait until later. "Good. Because Glen just admitted to killing all three of the victims. He's got Bree and me trapped in a shed and is firing at us."

Whitaker let out a curse. At least he was taking this seriously. "I'm probably twenty minutes out."

"Okay, we'll hold him off until then. Hurry." Tanner clicked off the phone.

He looked around. There was stuff piled up everywhere, but only one door. He moved away from the cover the piles of wood provided and eased toward the back of the shed. He wasn't going to wait for Glen to decide he was done talking and ready to start shooting. They'd be sitting ducks.

"Do you think my brother's really going to survive in a max security?" Glen yelled. "He can barely hack it at Camp George West. Those guys I killed gave up information on other people in order to get out of jail. They were scum. Criminals who then ratted out others in order to save themselves."

Tanner shifted a large metal shelf. Was that a small window up near the ceiling at the back? It had been blacked out, but maybe it would still open. It was going to make a lot of noise trying to get to it.

"Try to keep him talking so he can't hear me."

Bree nodded, watching him with wide eyes. She moved closer to the door.

"How did you know that they snitched on others?" she called out.

"The precious psychiatrist's files told me everything I needed to know. All three of them had to be cleared by Michalski before their sentences were reduced."

"What did you use to hack the files? Doxing? A Trojan horse or what?"

Tanner moved the large cabinet again, wincing as it made a loud scratching noise.

Meanwhile Bree looked like she was actually interested in how Glen had hacked the files. She probably was.

"Neither," Glen responded. "I did it the old-fashioned way. I bought the information from somebody else who hacked it. Michalski's own wife sold me the files."

"Why would she do that?" Bree whispered to Tanner. He had no idea, just continued to move furniture so he could get to the window.

"You want to know what the irony is?" Glen asked. His voice was sounding weary now. "I wrote, emailed and called Dr. Michalski for weeks, trying to get him to come evaluate Darin when we first got word of the transfer. Guy wouldn't even give me the time of day. You know how I met his wife? Because I was going to ask her if she might be willing to put in a good word with Michalski for us. We worked in the same building, but I didn't know her. It was my last shot."

While Glen continued to talk, Tanner finally muscled the furniture so that he could climb up it and reach the window.

Good news, it could be opened.

Bad news, there was no way he was going to fit through that. It was going to be tight, even for Bree.

"Ends up Mrs. Michalski hates her husband," Glen continued. "Evidently, he's been known to sleep with a patient a time or two. She couldn't put in a good word for me with him since she'd kicked him out of the house, but she was willing to give me his files for free so I could blackmail the good doctor into doing whatever I wanted."

"That would explain why Michalski was in the sheriff's office at 3:00 a.m. He probably doesn't have a home to go to right now," Tanner muttered as he pried open the window as wide as he could. Which still wasn't going to be large enough for him to fit, no matter how big he got it.

But at least Bree would be getting out.

"And did it work?" Bree yelled out. "Were you able to get Michalski to help you?"

"That bastard cop is just as bad as all the rest of the bastard cops. Didn't care about me. Didn't care about my brother or what would happen to him."

Glen's voice was clearer. He was getting closer.

"Tanner…" Bree whispered.

"I hear him. He's coming toward us. Climb up here."

She nodded but turned back to the door first.

"What about the emails? Why would you make your brother look guilty if you were trying to keep him out of the maximum-security prison?"

"I didn't do that!" Glen scoffed. "I would never do that. It must've been Michalski's way of making sure he didn't actually have to do what I want."

Tanner helped Bree climb up to where he was.

"I want you to go out the window."

She shook her head. "There's no way you're going to fit through that thing."

"I don't need to fit through. All we have to do is keep Glen talking until Whitaker gets here. He should be here in another ten or fifteen minutes."

They both knew Glen wasn't going to wait that long.

"But…"

He kissed her quickly. "Freckles, if there's going to be a shoot-out, it's better for me to be here by myself. Knowing you're undefended makes you vulnerable and splits my focus. By myself, I can keep him pinned. And—"

He stopped talking as a red electronic timer on the workshop table over Bree's shoulder blinked on. It hadn't been on a second ago.

And then it started counting down from two minutes.

"What the hell?" he muttered.

He let go of Bree and climbed down to take a closer look. She immediately followed. He traced the cord attached to the timer and lifted a greasy sheet that covered a large table. When he saw what it was attached to, his heart stopped.

The timer didn't.

"Oh my God," Bree whispered beside him. "Those are explosives."

Glen began yelling from outside again, much closer. "You shouldn't have come here, Dempsey. You weren't supposed to be here."

Tanner didn't waste any time. He grabbed Bree's arm and propelled her back up toward the window. "You have to get out, right now."

"But—"

"Situation is still the same. If I have to face Glen guns blazing, doing it by myself gives me a better chance."

"I don't want to leave you," she whispered.

"I know, freckles. But do it anyway."

She nodded.

Relief flooded his entire body. They didn't have time to fight this out. Knowing she was safe would allow him to focus. He kissed her hard once more then hoisted her up and through the impossibly small window.

"Get out of the blast range and stay hidden until Whitaker gets here," he told her as she wiggled her hips through. Once she made it, he winced as she fell forward. It was a long way to fall and no good way to catch herself.

But at least she'd be alive.

He couldn't see out the window to make sure she

was all right, but it wouldn't have mattered anyway—he was running out of time. Only forty-five seconds left on the countdown. If he had more time, he might have tried to call in support and see if there was any way he could disarm it, but there was no way that could happen now.

"Why are you doing this, Glen?" he called out. "It doesn't need to be this way."

He didn't actually expect Carrico to answer, but he did. "This wasn't what I wanted. Any of it. I just hope it's worth it in the end."

Tanner was done with the cryptic statements from this guy. He wasn't waiting any longer. Bree was safe.

He shot at the front window once to try to get Glen's attention focused in that direction, and then he stormed the door.

Chapter Twenty-Three

She and Tanner really were going to need to have a long talk about exactly what it meant to be a *team*. Team did not mean one person stayed in jeopardy while the other ran for her life.

But when the clock was ticking and some sort of bomb was about to blow up the whole building, it wasn't time for an argument. So she kissed him and wiggled out that tiny window and fell what felt like a thousand feet to the ground.

But she damn well didn't run to safety. Instead she immediately grabbed the biggest stick she could find and headed around to the front of the shed.

If Tanner was coming out of there guns blazing, then she was going to help him by coming from the back, club swinging.

As she sprinted around the building, Glen's attention was caught by the front window of the shed shattering. She ran as fast as she could toward the skinny man, even as Tanner came bursting out of the shed door, firing his gun in Glen's direction.

Glen was hit by one of Tanner's bullets, but only in the arm, not enough to take him down. And then he was firing, too. Tanner, out of bullets, dived to the side to get away from the shots firing his way.

She knew it wasn't going to be enough.

"No!" She screamed to get Glen's attention before he could fire at Tanner again and continued to run at full speed, branch raised.

Glen spun around to face her, and she knew he was going to get the shot off before she could hit him. She prepared herself for the feel of a bullet, but when the shot rang out, no pain came.

Instead, it was Glen who fell from a shot to the head. Bree spun to see what had happened. Did Tanner have another bullet she didn't know about? He was running toward her, leaping over Glen's body and pulling her against his chest and behind one of the larger trees.

Not two seconds later, the shed exploded, sending pieces of wood and metal flying out as shrapnel. The tree saved them from it ripping into their bodies.

Tanner held her away from him and looked down at her, fear clouding his brown eyes. "Are you okay?" He began patting her down, looking for wounds.

"I'm fine. How…? Did you shoot him?"

"Excuse me. Can I get a little help over here?" The voice was coming from the other side of where the shed had stood. They both rushed over through the smoke and debris to find Ryan Fletcher leaning up against a tree, gun next to him.

"Fletcher? What the hell are you doing here?" Tanner rushed to his friend's side and helped ease him to the ground.

"I was on my cell phone with Sheriff Duggan when Whitaker called in what was going on. I was closer, so I rushed over here. Made it just in time to shoot someone I've never met then get blown to kingdom come." He smiled. "Everybody always says an attorney's job is bloody."

Tanner smiled. "Well, you don't have any projectiles sticking out of your body, so I think you're going to be okay. Maybe a concussion."

"Pretty sure you've punched me harder than this, sparring."

Bree reached down and squeezed his shoulder. "You saved my life. Thank you."

"Anytime. I'm glad you guys don't have to run anymore." He smiled and leaned back against the tree.

About ten minutes later, Whitaker finally showed up, just in time to be of no real use whatsoever. An ambulance came for Ryan, but he refused to leave, even though he probably needed to get a CT scan.

Tanner stayed glued to Bree's side, and to be honest, she didn't want him far anyway. They'd come too close to losing each other.

They waited with Ryan on Glen's rickety front porch steps as some of the other sheriff's deputies arrived—including Ronnie Kitchens, who hugged them both—and began searching the house.

Whitaker came out a few minutes later. "Well, as far as I'm concerned, you're cleared, Dempsey. We found access to a huge stack of Dr. Michalski's files on Carrico's computer, cross-referenced with a list of all the people who'd gotten reduced sentences because of giving up info on others. Looks like Carrico planned to take them all out."

"Unbelievable," Ryan muttered.

"Would've liked to have known why he chose me to set up for the fall," Tanner said.

Bree pulled him closer. "And how he could possibly think this would help his brother's case. If anything, this will just make it harder for Darin to stay at the minimum-security facility."

"Guy had cancer, right?" Ryan asked. "He's pretty young. That couldn't have been easy. Maybe he just snapped."

"I guess so." Tanner rubbed his eyes then looked up at Whitaker. "You already knew about this place when I called. How'd you figure it out?"

"Michalski. I found him after you broke into the sheriff's office last night and locked him in that closet." He shot a sideways look at Bree. "After I figured out that the window alarm was false, of course. Michalski was just spitting mad that you had snuck into the building."

Tanner raised a dark eyebrow. "Didn't make *you* mad that I had snuck into the building?"

Whitaker leaned against the porch rail. "Don't get me wrong—I would've arrested your ass if I had caught you there. But I also couldn't think of many reasons you would be there at all if you were guilty and on the run."

Tanner shrugged. "I wasn't guilty."

"What I couldn't easily figure out was why *Michalski* was there at three in the morning. Started checking building logs, and it seemed he'd been there all night for multiple nights. Started looking further and figured out there was a lot going on with the doctor that he wasn't telling. I went to the sheriff, and she and I confronted him this morning with our concerns. He admitted his wife was divorcing him and had hacked his files. She'd been selling them to whoever she thought could do the most damage to Michalski's reputation."

"He should've been up front about that from the beginning," Bree said. "There were ways to do damage control. Hell, I could've tracked down anyone she'd sold the info to and destroyed it."

Whitaker nodded. "I think Michalski understands that. He's the one on administrative leave now. I'm sure you'll be reinstated as soon as the sheriff sees you, between what we found here, Carrico admitting to the killings and Fletcher finding him in the middle of attempted murder."

Tanner stood. "Good. Then the sheriff can expect to see me first thing tomorrow. Right now, we're going home."

Home. That was definitely where she wanted to go. She wanted to check on Star and Corfu and make sure they were doing okay. She wanted to sleep for a hundred hours in Tanner's big bed.

Beside him.

Bree and Ryan stood with him. Bree's grin was huge, Ryan's a little more painful as he rubbed his head. But he slapped Tanner on his back. "Congrats, buddy. I'm glad you're no longer the hunted. I'm going to help make sure the people who really deserve the blame for this get what's coming to them."

Tanner shook his head. "No, nobody in the department is to blame. It was just some unfortunate circumstances. I'm just ready to get back to the job."

Bree squeezed his hand. "And I know Risk Peak wants you back, too."

Ryan nodded. "If you say so. I think I'm going to take a few dozen aspirin and call it a day. I'll catch you guys later."

Tanner and Bree headed toward their car, too. Tanner still hadn't let go of her.

She smiled at him. "Looks like you get to go back to being Captain Sexy Li—"

She never finished the sentence as his mouth slammed against hers and he backed her against the car. She moaned, gripping at his hair and clutching him to her, totally not caring that his colleagues might be able to see them.

When they finally broke apart, he leaned his forehead against hers.

"You scared me to death. You're not great at following directions, you know that? You were supposed to run to safety. Not charge a fully-armed man with just a tree branch."

"Well, you're not great at understanding the whole concept of *team*. In a team, one person doesn't run for safety while the other gets riddled with bullet holes or blown to smithereens. So how about we call it even?"

He smiled. "How about we go home?"

"Sounds perfect to me."

Chapter Twenty-Four

"You know you don't have to do this. I know we joked about it when we were on the run, but I never actually expected us to go on any sort of romantic getaway."

Tanner reached over and grabbed both Bree's hands that were wringing nervously in her lap. He brought one to his lips.

"I wanted to do this. Wanted to take you somewhere romantic and secluded. And where I didn't have to compete for your attention with a certain dog and her pups."

The case had been closed now for nearly a week. Dr. Michalski was on extended administrative leave while law enforcement got the rest of the hacked-files situation under control.

Darin Carrico had been devastated by his brother's death, but true to his word, Tanner had looked into the situation surrounding Darin's sudden prison transfer. Once he started questioning it, nobody seemed to be able to provide a real reason for why the transfer was occurring. Tanner made a special request, and with the help of Ryan Fletcher, it looked like Darin was going to be able to stay at Camp George West for the remainder of his sentence.

It seemed a waste for four people to die in order to make something happen that should've happened with just a phone call.

Bree reached over to cup his cheek. "Hey, what's that frown about?"

He turned his head so he could kiss her palm, loving the way she pushed her own discomfort aside because she was worried about him. "Nothing. Just thinking about how all this could've been avoided if Darin and Glen had felt like someone would listen to them. None of this had to happen."

She nodded. "I wish it hadn't happened this way. Even though the dead guys were criminals, they still didn't deserve to die. And the thought of Glen being so desperate… I feel like he only became a killer because he was backed into a corner."

"Yeah. Under different circumstances, his life would not have ended up this way. And I'm going to try to help Darin as much as I can once he gets out. God knows that family needs some proof that not all law enforcement is bad. Maybe I can help him get a job. Get visitation with his daughter."

It was the least he could do, because if the system hadn't been broken in the first place, all this might have been avoided.

She nodded. "Good. Because he's going to be lost

without Glen. But still, I can't help but be glad there are a few good things that came from all this."

"Like what?"

"Like the fact that you and I might have danced around your PTSD for months before we talked about it outright. It could've festered and grown into something a lot more difficult to surmount."

"You're definitely right about that."

She nodded. "And of course helping Darin, like you said. Everybody needs a way to be heard. Speaking of, I talked to Cassandra about the computer class she wants me to teach for the shelter. I've decided to do it. To teach it myself."

He grinned. He'd known it was just a matter of time until she'd come around. "I think you'll be great at it."

She shrugged. "If they can find the guts to leave their abusive situations, certainly I can find the guts to help teach these incredible women a new skill."

"Have I told you how absolutely amazing you are?"

She grinned and waggled her eyebrows. "I'm hoping maybe we can take this weekend and both find some ways to show each other that."

Sheriff Duggan had insisted Tanner take the entire weekend off. He'd been working twelve- and fifteen-hour days since he'd been reinstated. Just the paperwork involved with everything that had happened had been a full-time job, plus everything that had fallen through the cracks while he'd been away.

The sheriff hadn't needed to twist Tanner's arm to take a whole weekend off. He'd been more than happy for two full days to devote to Bree. He'd barely seen her all week. Except for the night immediately after Glen's death, when he'd taken them to the ranch, they'd both been staying at their own places in Risk Peak.

But he planned to talk to her about moving in with him by the time the weekend was over. He wanted her with him.

They pulled up at the resort in Estes Park—an ornate place with remote bungalows meant specifically for romance and privacy.

He hadn't told Bree where they were going, and her eyes grew big now as they parked and walked inside the main lodge to get their key. "Wow, this is fancy."

He pulled her up against him. "You deserve fancy."

She deserved *everything*.

The sun was setting as they checked in and walked down the lovely path that led to their private bungalow.

"It's a different view from the ranch, but the ranch is gorgeous in its own way," she said. "Maybe you guys ought to consider opening a resort."

He chuckled. "Noah would love that. He says I already owe him a week's worth of winter chores for having to spend three hours in the sheriff department's interrogation room avoiding answering questions about me."

She laughed. "You know he's going to wait until the middle of a blizzard and then call in his marker."

"I have no doubt about it."

He opened the door and escorted her inside with his hand at the small of her back.

"Man, this place really is *bougie*."

He raised an eyebrow. "*Bougie?* Is that bad or good?"

"Do you not ever talk to any of the teenagers in town? They taught it to me. *Bougie* is fancy good. I finally researched its origins and found out it's from the word *bourgeois*."

He shook his head. "I'm obviously not up on my slang. I'll work on that."

Once they were both inside and had looked around the bedroom and the living area with windows that opened out to a stunning view, Tanner wasn't exactly sure what to do.

He'd brought her here to make love to her. Because he wanted the first time to be absolutely perfect for her, to make up for everything she'd gone through in the last week.

He hadn't let himself get too close to her this week because he hadn't wanted their first time to be rushed or ordinary. He wanted it to be...*bougie*.

He'd wanted to make love to her for so long, but now that the time was here, with no obstacles in their way and in a wondrous, romantic spot, he was actually a little nervous.

"I'm not sure what I'm supposed to say right now," she said. "Is everything okay? We don't have to do anything if you're not ready."

Enough. His own indecision was making *her* nervous. He snagged her around the waist and pulled her up against him. "Isn't that supposed to be my line?"

She smiled, winding her arms around his shoulders. "It's been a long week for you. And I know it all turned out okay in terms of your job, but we don't have to do anything tonight if it's just not the right time."

"An isolated room with a giant bed and nobody interrupting us? Oh, I think this very definitely *is* the right time for you and me."

His lips had barely touched hers when the phone rang on the bedside table. He ignored it, much more interested in the feel of Bree's lips than whatever was going to be said on the phone.

But when it kept ringing, Bree finally wiggled away from him and answered it herself.

"Hello?" He continued to kiss down her neck as she answered. He could hear the voice speaking briskly.

"So sorry to interrupt you, Mrs. Dempsey. This is the front desk."

"I'm not Mrs. Dempsey, but I'm here with Mr. Dempsey." Tanner loved how she was breathing hard and struggled to get the words out as he continued to kiss her neck.

"My apologies. We have a bottle of champagne, for the Dempsey party, courtesy of the Grand County Sheriff's Department, waiting for you at the front desk. We would normally deliver it to your room, but our bellboy just got sick and had to go home."

"That's okay. I'll walk up and get it." She squeaked out the last word as he bit down lightly on the side of her neck.

She barely got the phone back in its cradle before he had her pulled up against him. Her arm reached back, fingers threading into his hair, throat tilting back as she leaned her head on his shoulder, giving him better access.

Her back was completely pressed up against his front. He used one hand to keep her neck tilted at the angle he wanted, and the other to find all the places on the front of her body that he could play with until she gasped.

He found many.

And didn't stop until she was bucking against his hand and calling out his name.

"You stay here, and I'll go get the champagne," he whispered in her ear as she finally caught her breath and recovered from the shudders racking her body.

She turned and snuggled against him like a little cat, rubbing his chest with her nose. He loved to see her so sated and happy like this.

And the weekend was just getting started.

"No," she whispered. "I'll get it. I know you wanted to shower. You get going on that, and be ready when I get back with the champagne." She slipped away from him. "You better hurry, because if you're not done, I'm going to have to join you in there."

He pulled her in for a quick kiss. "You're going to have to work on your threatening skills."

"Oh yeah?" she asked. "Then how about this as a threat?"

He nearly swallowed his tongue as she whispered some of the things she planned to do to him once they were both naked.

"But I need a couple of sips of champagne first," she finished with a smile.

"Good gravy, woman. Hurry up and get that champagne."

The sound of her laugh as she ran toward the door ranked right up there with his favorite things on the planet.

He made a beeline for the shower, because although he wouldn't mind her joining him in there, that could wait. The first time they made love, he wanted it to be in a bed, where he could take his time.

For just a second, he had a moment's pause. Their first time really should've been in his bed back at the ranch—where everything started for them. But he shook it off. There would be plenty of time to make love to her there, too.

He was out of the shower five minutes later and slipping on the sleep pants he'd brought but had no plans to be sleeping in and walked back into the bedroom. No Bree.

It was only after another ten minutes had passed that he began to get concerned.

He picked up the phone on the bedside table and dialed the front desk. "Did anybody come by yet to pick up the bottle of champagne left for the Dempsey party?"

He could hear papers shuffling around before the woman at the front desk answered. "I'm sorry, sir. I just arrived for my shift. Can you give me just a moment and I'll call you right back with an update?"

"Sure." He hung up.

Had Bree gotten lost on the path to the front desk? It was a pretty straight shot, but she had been known to get distracted by things. He wasn't worried, but he'd just go look for her. He slipped on a shirt and pair of shoes.

He saw the envelope as soon as he came out of the bedroom. The bloodred color of it was almost garish against the snowy white of the rug it lay on. Tanner tore it open.

Bungalow 42. I have a surprise for you.

What the hell? What in the world had Bree done? Had she figured out where he was going to take her—not that that would be difficult for her, since he'd put the reservation on his credit card—and had planned something of her own?

This woman kept him on his toes, that was for sure.

Ironically, bungalow 42 was the one he'd wanted. It was the most isolated, with the very best view. But it had already been booked.

Tanner smiled. Looked like now he was going to get it anyway.

He slipped out the door. Of course, if Bree had hacked his credit card account, they were going to have to have a long talk.

But first they were going to have a long time *not talking*.

He half jogged to the outskirts of the property, smiling the entire time. His grin grew bigger when he saw the door was cracked open and candles lit inside. Who would've thought Bree would have her own romantic side.

He pushed the door open. "Freckles, you are in so much trouble. I'm going to show you how to—"

Tanner stopped talking when he heard a voice from the far corner, obviously not Bree's.

"Dempsey. I thought for a second I had misplayed this, that you weren't going to come."

Ryan? What in the hell was going on?

"What are you doing here, man?"

In the dim light of the candles, he could see Ryan reach over for a light switch on the wall. "It's a little dark in here, isn't it?" Ryan asked. "Let me shed a little light on the subject."

He flipped a switch, and all the oxygen was sucked out of Tanner's world when he saw Bree, strung up by her neck, struggling to keep stable on a chair balancing precariously on its back legs.

"Does this situation feel familiar at all?"

Chapter Twenty-Five

Fear was a fist in Tanner's throat, blocking his airway. He let out a vile curse. "What the hell is going on here, Fletcher?"

Tanner rushed toward them, but Fletcher pulled out a knife and held it against Bree's ribs. "No farther, or she'll be dead before she hits the floor. Oh, wait—she won't hit the floor. She'll just dangle there in the air."

Tanner stopped his approach. He didn't want to tip her balance in the chair or cause Ryan to do anything to hurt her further.

"Fine." He held his hands out in front of him in a gesture of surrender, wishing desperately he'd brought his weapon.

Bree's arms were restrained behind her back, and there was a piece of industrial tape covering her mouth. Her beautiful green eyes were wide and frantic as she struggled to keep her balance with her toes on the chair.

Yes, this was a very familiar scene, and Tanner knew exactly what she was going through.

"Hang in there, freckles," he said in a low voice.

Ryan laughed, the sound cruel and ugly. "*Hang in there?* That's a pretty poor choice of words if you're trying to provide her any comfort."

"I don't know what kind of sick game you're playing, but it ends now. Cut. Her. Down."

Fletcher's handsome face contorted into a sneer. "No, I don't think so. Not after all the trouble I went through to get us to this place. I think it's about time that you learned what it's like to lose someone."

Tanner's body twitched with the need to move as Ryan took the point of his knife and ran it down Bree's bare arm.

"My original plan involved you rotting in prison for a few life sentences, but it didn't take me very long to realize how deeply you have everyone fooled. Everyone in this entire damn county thinks that you're some sort of hero. They have no understanding of what you really are—a murderer."

Tanner tried to wrap his head around what Ryan was saying, while keeping his eyes glued to Bree's face. "I didn't kill those guys. Glen Carrico admitted to it."

Ryan shook his head. "Glen Carrico had about twenty-three more seconds to live and was willing to do whatever he could to keep his baby brother from being transferred to big-boy prison. I was happy to scratch Carrico's back if he scratched mine."

It was all starting to make sense to Tanner. "*You* are behind the whole thing from the beginning. Did you kill Anders, Newkirk and Duquette yourself?"

Tanner grimaced when Ryan gave the chair Bree was balancing on a little push, causing her to rock haphazardly. Tears squeezed out of her panicked eyes.

He made his peace right then and there that he was going to have to kill a man he thought was his friend.

And he wasn't going to hesitate.

He let out the breath he'd been holding as Bree finally found her balance again. He knew the terror she was going through. Knew how tired the muscles in her legs would be from trying to hold her weight at an awkward angle and just on her toes. It wouldn't be long before her calves would begin to cramp and seize.

He could feel the phantom noose around his own throat like it was yesterday.

"Yeah, I killed them." Ryan raised an eyebrow. "So what? The world should thank me for removing people like them from the streets. Hell, you were the one who stated outright that they should stay in jail."

"But that didn't mean I thought they should be killed."

Ryan shrugged one shoulder carelessly. "They were just a means to an end, anyway. Their deaths were supposed to be your fall from grace. But nobody was willing to believe the great and mighty Tanner Dempsey could possibly be the bad guy."

There was no point in trying to argue that Tanner hadn't actually killed anyone and that was why no one believed him capable of it.

"Why are you doing this, Ryan? Because of Nate? Why now? You and I have been hanging out for years."

"And never once during that time did you mention the fact that if you would've broken that rope around your neck sooner—tried a little harder—you could've saved Nate's life."

It all became clear to Tanner.

"You got into Dr. Michalski's hacked files." That had to be it. Besides Noah and Bree, Michalski was the only other person he'd talked about Nate's death with.

And he'd said those very words. Felt that very guilt. That if he'd just made an effort and snapped the rope sooner, he could've stopped Nate from being shot.

"Michalski's files are what brought Carrico and me together. All the times I talked with you, I always thought you had done everything you could to save Nate. That you weren't to be blamed. But I was wrong, wasn't I? You are to be blamed, yet no one ever did. Not even so much as a mark on your file."

"Ryan—"

"Don't try to talk your way out of this. Don't forget I've had plenty of time watching you work people on the stands. I used to admire you for it, how smooth you were. But that was before I realized that you were a murderer. Then it was like my blinders were ripped off and I could finally see you for what you really were—an egotistical bastard who thinks he's better than everyone."

"Ryan, please believe me. I would've saved your brother if I could've—"

"Liar!"

Tanner watched in horror as Ryan pulled the chair out from under Bree's outstretched leg. Without its support, she fell forward and the rope began to strangle her. She began to flail, her body instinctively trying to do whatever it could to ease the pressure on her throat and allow oxygen in.

Tanner rushed toward them but stopped when Ryan brought the knife tip up to the side of Bree's neck. The way she was jerking caused her to jab herself into it. Blood soon began trickling down her throat.

"Stop, or she dies this second."

"Get the chair back under her legs, right damn now." Tanner could feel every muscle in his body tensed to attack. Could he get to Ryan before he dealt Bree a fatal blow with a knife?

He relaxed the slightest bit when Ryan pulled the knife away from her neck and placed the chair back under her legs.

The pressure was off her throat now, but she was still panicking, unable to breathe under the tape.

"Ryan, take that tape off her mouth."

Bree's chest was moving at a way too rapid pace

for the amount of oxygen she was able to get in. She was going to hyperventilate, and that would be deadly in her current state. Passing out might lower her breathing rate, but it would also mean she couldn't keep her balance on the chair.

"Freckles," he said, trying to keep the panic out of his voice. "Look at me. You can do this."

He didn't even know if she heard him. Her eyes were still wild and darting all around the room, her chest heaving.

"Goddamn it, Ryan, if she passes out, you won't have any leverage over me whatsoever." And Tanner was damn well going to kill him. "Take the tape off *now*."

Ryan let out an annoyed sigh. "Fine." He reached up and ripped the tape brutally off her face.

Bree flinched, then began sucking in big gulps of air. They weren't out of danger yet. The oxygen now flooding her system could make her just as dizzy.

"Freckles, I need you to slow down your breathing. If you pass out, there's nothing to keep you balanced on that chair. Look at me."

Those green eyes finally settled on his face. She watched him, and he took slow breaths with her, getting her to match his. "That a girl. You're amazing."

Ryan just watched the entire exchange, shaking his head. "You know, *she* is the reason I really couldn't tolerate this anymore. It's bad enough that you fooled everyone who knows you into thinking you're some sort of hero. Then you actually get to fall in love? Have a wonderful future with someone? Nate didn't get to have that. So it was totally unacceptable to me that you would."

"So your grand plan was to frame me for murder?"

"It wasn't enough just to kill you." Ryan was so angry, spittle flew from his mouth as he spoke. "The world needed to know the truth about you. That you're the enemy and to be feared, not to be revered."

Tanner took a slight step closer. He needed to keep Ryan distracted long enough to be in diving range. And he had to be able to tackle him from an angle that would lead him away from Bree.

"I guess I played right into your hands by running. That was a nice touch."

Ryan shrugged. "It definitely would've been more difficult to pin all this on you if you had been there to answer all their questions. It's so ridiculous how much people wanted to believe you were innocent."

"Even Whitaker?" Tanner took another slight step forward. He wanted to look at Bree, to reassure her, but he knew he needed to keep Ryan's attention focused on him.

"Especially Whitaker. I thought for sure that guy wouldn't be blinded by your halo since he's not from around here, but he fell for your lies just as much as everyone else."

Ryan wasn't actually interested in the truth. Whitaker didn't like Tanner much at all, and he definitely wasn't blind to Tanner's faults. If Tanner had been the real killer, Whitaker wouldn't have hesitated for a second to take him down. But all Ryan could see were the lies he'd convinced himself of.

"So when it became apparent I wasn't going to be able to convince the people around here of your deceit and depravity, I decided I had to change my tactics. I wouldn't have the joy of seeing you rot in prison for the rest of your life, but I could still put Nate's ghost to rest by killing you."

"Then kill me. But leave Bree out of this. She has nothing to do with you, me, Nate or any of it."

"Tanner…"

Hearing her shredded voice absolutely gutted him. It had been weeks before his own voice had recovered from his ordeal. Weeks of not being able to swallow without pain.

Ryan turned to her but thankfully didn't move the chair again. "Did you know your boyfriend was a murderer? Did you know that if he just tried a little harder he could've saved my brother's life? That Nate would still be here?"

"No," Bree whispered.

Tanner took another step forward while Ryan was focused on her.

"Yes! He said so to Dr. Michalski himself."

"The things he said to Michalski are his worst fears, not the actual truth. He said them because he blames himself." Her voice was soft but steady. "He's spent hours of his life trying to figure out if it would've made a difference if he had pulled on that rope harder earlier. Sometimes he can't sleep at night knowing that if things had been different—just the slightest bit different—your brother would still be here."

"He should have tried harder!" Ryan screamed.

"Tanner would be the first person to tell you that. But you know what he wouldn't tell you?"

Tanner was about to take another step, but he froze just in time as Ryan looked back at him. "There's a hell of a lot he wouldn't tell me. Stuff he's left out for years."

"Well, I'll tell you something he wouldn't tell you. He wouldn't tell me, either, but I hacked the hospital files to see how badly he'd been hurt. Do you know that Tanner was tortured for hours to get him to give up the other police officers he was working with? Do you know that your brother didn't die in agony because Tanner took all that punishment on himself and never cracked? Broken bones, burns, knife wounds. Did your brother have any of those, Ryan? If not, it's because Tanner took everyone's share."

He hadn't wanted her to know those details, hadn't wantēd for her to be responsible for carrying them. But once again he'd been underestimating what she could handle.

The woman who argued she had no interpersonal skills certainly seemed to have them now. Ryan was actually listening to her. Maybe there would be a way out of this without someone leaving in a body bag.

And he would take up the hospital file hacking with her later.

He got another step closer before Ryan turned to look at him again. "Is she telling the truth?"

"I didn't want anybody to die that day. But honestly, I didn't think there was any chance I was walking out of there alive. The Viper Syndicate already knew I was a cop. I figured if I could stop Nate and Alex from suffering the same fate, it was the best I could do."

"But they died. Nate died." Ryan's hand with the knife lowered. For the first time it seemed like he wanted to understand what had really happened.

But Bree's legs were shaking. She wasn't going to be able to support herself on that chair for much longer.

"Yes, they died. And part of that is always going to be my fault. Bree is right. It wakes me up at night, the fear that I could've done something differently that would've gotten those two men—especially Nate—out alive."

For a moment, Tanner really thought it was going to be enough. That the sensible man and razor-sharp lawyer he'd always known Ryan Fletcher to be was going to see reason and realize that what he was doing right now—hurting Bree—was desperately wrong.

But then something flickered in his mind. Tanner could almost see the exact moment when the anger or bitterness or sheer madness—whatever it was—overcame his friend again.

"No," Ryan said, knife coming up in his hand once

more. "You don't get to talk your way out of this with your charming swagger. You don't get to live while Nate doesn't. You don't get to have a happily-ever-after with a beautiful woman while he rots in the ground. You're going to know what it's like to watch her die, and then you're going to die your—"

Tanner didn't wait for him to finish. He knew what was coming next—Ryan had just announced it. Instead, Tanner launched himself at Ryan as hard as he could.

He was coming in from too far, at the wrong angle, but at least that knife was nowhere close to Bree. Instead it sliced straight into Tanner's shoulder as he crashed into Ryan, sending them both rolling to the ground.

Tanner grunted through the pain as Ryan pulled out the knife to try to stab him again with it.

He caught Ryan's wrist on the downward swing, stopping the knife from where it would've landed in his jugular. He threw his weight to the side, trying to roll Ryan with him, farther from Bree. But they had sparred too many times and Ryan was too well aware of his tactics to be taken by surprise.

Instead, Ryan pushed in the opposite direction, bringing the blade down and catching Tanner on the biceps.

He ignored the burn of the new cut, clocking Ryan in the jaw with his elbow before spinning around and catching him in the face again with an uppercut.

Ryan was dazed but didn't let go of the knife. Both

men got to their feet, staring at each other, ready to do battle. Tanner knew it wasn't just his life he was fighting for. If Ryan took him out, he would definitely kill Bree, too.

Tanner braced himself for another attack with the knife, his mind working out possible scenarios based on what he knew about Ryan's fighting style. Ryan wasn't as strong as Tanner, but he was deadly fast and eerily precise in his strikes. In a fistfight that made them just about even. But the knife in Ryan's hand definitely gave him an advantage, not to mention the wounds that were already dripping blood everywhere and would soon be slowing Tanner down.

But the lightning blows he'd expected never came. Instead, Ryan pivoted and slid to the side of Tanner. Tanner quickly caught him, but not before the other man threw out his leg in a slide kick and knocked over the chair Bree was balancing on.

He could hear Bree's strangled groans behind him as the rope once again cut off her source of oxygen. Tanner dived for the chair, but Ryan tackled him, knocking him out of the way.

He felt the sting of the knife again and again as he threw Ryan off him and crawled toward Bree. His side. His calf. Tanner kicked out blindly behind him as his fingers brushed the leg of the wooden chair. He just needed a few more inches and he'd be able to right it back under her.

Then he couldn't stop his cry of pain when the

knife stabbed him deep in his waist. Unlike the other blows that had been slices, this one had done definite damage.

The whole room was starting to get a little fuzzy around the edges. Tanner was losing too much blood. He didn't have much time.

He was working at a disadvantage because Ryan was using Bree against him as a weakness. As a chink in his armor. As long as Tanner kept trying to protect her, Ryan had Tanner exactly where he wanted him.

But if there was anything the last couple of weeks had taught him, it was that Bree was his partner. She was nobody's liability.

They were a team. She'd said it herself.

His fingers wrapped around the edge of the chair again. He knew Ryan expected him to crawl toward her with it, to try to get it back under her.

But Bree was strong. She could make it. And that wasn't something Ryan had taken into consideration.

Instead of moving toward her, Tanner spun with the chair in hand and slammed it against Ryan's head. Caught completely off guard, the man fell to the ground, dazed.

Once Ryan was down, Tanner stumbled the couple of feet toward her, lifting Bree's weight by her thighs, taking the pressure off her throat.

She sucked in a couple of gulps of air then croaked out, "Finish him."

She had to know Tanner would need to let her

go to do that. Even setting her back down as gently as he could, it was the hardest thing he'd ever done.

This time she didn't flail as her oxygen cut back off. She trusted him to do what he had to do.

He trusted her to survive as he did it.

A team.

Tanner turned back toward Ryan, reaching down and grabbing a leg of the chair that had broken. Ryan was starting to recover from the blow to the head, but it wasn't enough.

Ryan spun the knife toward Tanner again, but with one blow of the chair leg, it went flying from his hand. Three blows with the chair leg later, and Ryan was unconscious on the ground. The sickening thud from the third blow probably meant Tanner had broken his jaw or cracked his skull.

Tanner didn't care. Ryan was down and was going to stay down.

Tanner took a step toward the knife, his foot sliding in whatever liquid was covering the ground. He let out a low curse when he realized the liquid was blood, most of it his.

The room was spinning, his vision reduced to a pinprick now. He fought to hold on to consciousness and knew if he didn't get that knife and get Bree cut down, she would strangle there.

That was damn well not going to happen.

He got the knife and tried to crawl back to her, but everything had turned so dark he couldn't seem to find her.

"Tanner." Her voice was a hoarse whisper, but it was enough.

He forced himself to his feet and took drunken steps toward her. "Freckles?"

"Tanner."

He wasn't sure if it was her voice that led him to her or sheer blind luck. But he ran into her hanging form a moment later.

Using the last of his strength, he lifted her. There was no way he was going to be able to cut the rope from her neck. It was all he could do to stay upright.

After a moment of breathing, she whispered, "Just cut my hands, baby. I'll do the rest."

He couldn't see the tape on her wrists, couldn't see anything at all. He just prayed he wasn't cutting her too badly as he kept one arm wrapped around her legs, supporting her weight, and used the other to slice through the tape.

"You did it," she whispered. She took the knife from his hands. "We can do this, Tanner. You've always held me up, in every possible way. Now just do it for a couple more minutes."

Her voice seemed like it was coming from a great distance, but no matter what, he would do it.

"Won't let go." His words sounded mumbled and unintelligible, even to his own ears. But she understood.

"I know you won't."

He drew on every iota of strength he had to hold her weight while she cut herself down. In the end it was thoughts of Nate, and the rope he would've sworn he didn't have the strength to break and yet had, that kept him in place.

Sometimes you didn't know how strong you were until strong was the only option you had left.

He felt Bree's weight collapse against him and knew she'd managed to cut through the rope. They both fell to the ground, tangled with each other.

And the black that he'd fought for so long consumed him.

Chapter Twenty-Six

All Bree could do for the first few moments after falling to the ground with Tanner was breathe.

Every breath seemed to stab her lungs like a blade, but at least she had air. He'd saved her, by finding the superhuman strength to support her while she hacked at the rope.

"Tanner!" She yelled his name when he didn't move at all, but the sound was barely more than a whisper. She felt for a pulse, sobbing silently in relief when she found one.

The bungalow floor was covered with so much of his blood. Way too much of it. She didn't want to leave him for a second but knew she had to get help here as soon as possible. She crawled over to the phone and called the front desk, screaming as loudly as she could—which still meant they could barely hear her—for them to call for an ambulance.

She struggled back to him, forcing down the panic every time she slipped in his blood, and pulled his unconscious form into her arms, holding pressure on his wounds as best she could. There were so, so many.

She was going to lose him.

She struggled so often with finding the proper emotions for a situation. But not this time. This time she knew exactly what she felt: mind-crushing fear.

But his heart kept beating. She whispered everything she could think of in his ear as she held him waiting for the paramedics to arrive. Promises of everything she wanted to do with him. Marry him. Have babies with him. Travel the world but still always come home to the ranch. She wanted to be there with him when Star had puppies, and her puppies had puppies.

And she wanted sex. There was so much sex she wanted with him.

She told him over and over that she loved him and he was her hero.

When she ran out of promises, she moved on to threats. Threatening to illegally hack into every database in the country if he died and left her alone. To send secret messages to Whitaker about what she was doing so he would come arrest her.

Finally, after what seemed like an eternity, the paramedics arrived.

Letting them take Tanner from her was the hardest thing she'd ever done. How could she will his heart to continue beating if he was out of her sight? But she knew she had to let them take him. Help him.

"We are a team, Tanner Dempsey!" She was trying for a yell, but her ravaged voice came out as a croak. "It takes *both* of us to be a team."

A second set of paramedics insisted on looking at her wounds and refused to let her drive when she tried to stumble toward the door and get to Tanner's car. She wanted to scream at them to leave her alone, but her voice was completely useless by that point.

When they started talking about taking her to a different hospital than they'd taken Tanner, she began to panic. She couldn't communicate without her voice, and no one was willing to listen to what she was trying to say or figure out what she wanted.

She wanted to be near Tanner. She didn't care if the other hospital had strangled-people specialists. She had to be near Tanner. She could feel the agitation building at her inability to communicate. When her tears fell and she began to pull away from everyone, they thought she was in shock and started talking about sedating her.

As if she couldn't *hear* as well as couldn't speak.

Ironically, it was Whitaker, who showed up a few minutes later to help process the crime scene, who finally made the difference. He got down on the ground next to her where she sat, covered in Tanner's blood, and asked her what she needed.

Tanner. She mouthed it to him over and over until he finally nodded.

After Ryan was cuffed and taken away in his own ambulance, Whitaker left the crime scene to his colleagues, since it wasn't his jurisdiction anyway, and rode with Bree in the ambulance to the same hospital as Tanner.

The paramedics had once more tried to talk her into going to the other facility, but it was Whitaker who'd laid a hand on her shoulder and firmly told the paramedics no. So as far as she was concerned, Whitaker no longer held the status of ass hat.

Of course, he made her get checked out by the doctors before taking her to see Tanner, so he was still in the general ass vicinity. But maybe just jackass.

The doctor had checked out her throat, declared her very lucky to not have a crushed windpipe, announced it would take weeks of discomfort and blah, blah, blah, but that Bree should make a full recovery.

As soon as she knew her injuries weren't life-threatening, she'd demanded to use Whitaker's—whom she couldn't seem to get rid of now—phone and typed out one word.

Tanner.

She already knew her throat was in bad shape. She could feel the razor blades every time she swallowed or breathed too deeply. She'd wanted to be with Tanner. She agreed to let them admit her so they could treat her throat and help her manage the pain, as long as they agreed not to keep her from Tanner if he needed her.

She didn't even know if he was alive. Would someone have come and told her if he'd died? She began getting agitated again.

Whitaker sighed and procured a wheelchair to wheel her into the trauma waiting room, while Bree went into the bathroom and cleaned as much blood off herself as possible.

It wasn't until she was on her way into the waiting room that she wished she had her computer. They weren't going to let her near Tanner without being family. If she had her computer, she could've changed files and made herself such an ironclad member of his family—at least on the screen—that nobody in this hospital would dare keep her away from him.

It would've been illegal, but so worth it.

She didn't have to break any laws. When a nurse tried to tell Bree that this particular waiting area was for family only, Mrs. Dempsey, who was already there, stepped up and very clearly stated that Bree *was* family.

Noah and Cassandra echoing the sentiment brought tears to her eyes. She was saved from saying what would no doubt be the wrong thing by the fact that she couldn't talk anyway. All she could do was collapse into Mrs. Dempsey's arms as the older woman pulled her close.

"He's going to be just fine," Mrs. Dempsey whispered. "Just you watch. My boy has everything to live for now. He's not going to give that up."

Ended up she was right, although it didn't look like it for the first forty-eight hours.

After the first few hours of sitting in the waiting room, Bree's body was shaking with pain and fatigue. It was Noah who recognized it and came and squatted right in front of her, looking so much like Tanner it was a little painful.

"It's time for you to get checked into your own room and deal with your own injuries. I give you my word that if something happens with Tanner, for better or worse, I will personally carry you to him. Even if I have to knock some doctors and orderlies unconscious to do it. He's going to need you. This isn't going to be something he bounces back from right away. The best thing you can do to help him is to regather your strength while he's out."

Bree finally nodded. She was in a hospital room and pumped full of medications less than an hour later.

When she woke up the next morning, Dan and Cheryl were sitting in the room with her. She couldn't talk to them, but her eyes filled with tears once again when they explained that nobody in Risk Peak wanted her to be alone. A member of the Dempsey family came by and reported in once an hour, to let her know how Tanner was doing.

Stable, but not awake. Always stable, but not awake.

She borrowed Whitaker's phone when he came by again and backdoored her way into the hospital system. It wasn't that she didn't trust the Dempseys; she just had to see the information about Tanner for herself. Tanner's patient file basically said the same thing the Dempseys had been reporting, but in medical jargon: stable, but not awake.

On the second day, when Tanner started to stir but not quite wake, he mumbled Bree's name. True to his word, Noah was back in her room to get her and bring her to Tanner. Fortunately, he didn't have to knock anyone unconscious, since she was doing so much better.

She rushed to Tanner's bed. "I'm here," she whispered.

She wrapped her fingers in his, and he immediately fell back into a more restful state.

He was in and out for two days after that. It was so obvious that he did better when Bree was around him—slept more deeply, had a more even heart rate and blood pressure—that the doctors didn't try to insist she not stay.

Every medical professional who had come in contact with him, from the paramedics to the surgeons, had stated that it was a miracle Tanner was even alive anyway. So the fact that his unconscious mind could seem to sense her presence, and his body rest and heal itself better with her near, seemed much less impressive, all things considered.

Bree was officially released from the hospital after two days. She'd stayed by Tanner's side the entire time except for when Cassandra, with the muscle of Noah, had forced Bree to go home to her apartment, take a shower and grab some clothes.

Bree and Cassandra had had plenty of hours to

talk—well, mostly Cassandra talked and Bree listened since she couldn't say more than a few sentences at a time—about plans for the shelter and the computer classes Bree could offer.

Cassandra wanted to start the classes as soon as possible. Bree, not even counting her voice, wasn't quite so gung ho. But like Cassandra said, the skills and hope they were providing these women couldn't wait. Bree's discomfort wasn't what was important.

"Of course, we'll wait until you can speak louder than a whisper," Cassandra said with a smile from across Tanner's hospital room. "You're probably a more effective instructor if people can actually hear you."

"Don't rush her," Mrs. Dempsey said. She'd been a constant in Tanner's room every day. "Your brother is going to need someone to take care of him for a while. Let them get themselves situated and then you can drag her into all your grand schemes."

"I know, Mom, and I don't expect her to do it until she's ready and healed." Cassandra winked at her. "So what is that, like two or three days?"

Bree just smiled.

"Bree, speaking of Tanner getting out of here… I don't want you to feel like you have to take him on all by yourself if you don't want to. I can assure you that my son is not a good patient. He doesn't like to stay in bed."

"I'll bet Bree will be a little better at keeping

him in bed," Cassandra muttered under her breath with a grin.

Bree could feel heat rising through her whole face.

Mrs. Dempsey didn't look offended, thank goodness. "My obnoxious daughter may be right, but I still don't want you to feel like you have to be responsible for him. We can certainly all take turns."

Bree stared at Mrs. Dempsey, her heart feeling a little too big for her chest. Had she just been given first dibs on Tanner's care by his mother?

"I want to do it," she croaked out.

"Thank God," Cassandra muttered again. "He would've thrown a fit."

Bree wasn't exactly sure that was the truth. "Let Tanner decide," she whispered.

Mrs. Dempsey and Cassandra looked at each other before looking back at Bree. "Believe me, if it was up to my son, he would've moved you in to the ranch the day he returned to Risk Peak. He wants you there. He wanted you there back when he thought you might be a package deal with two sweet babies."

"Oh." Bree's lips formed the word, but no sound came out.

"So before you say yes, that you'll move in and take care of him, I want to make sure you understand exactly what you're getting yourself into. Once you move your stuff and yourself onto that ranch, it will be for good. Tanner's never going to let you go."

"Oh." Again, no sound. Bree wanted to believe

Mrs. Dempsey's words more than anything she'd ever known.

Mrs. Dempsey got up from her chair near the window and came to stand next to Bree, who was sitting near the sleeping Tanner, holding his hand. "You have some doubts left about how he feels, and that's okay. He'll clear them up for you."

"I just want to make sure it's what he really wants. I don't want him to feel pressured into anything."

She squeezed Bree's shoulder. "Is it what *you* want?"

Hiding her feelings wasn't even an option. She wasn't sure if sharing them with Tanner's mother was appropriate or not, but she couldn't hold back the words. "Yes. It's what I want. *He* is what I want. In every possible way."

Her words didn't need to be loud to be forceful.

Cassandra's low whistle and muttered "damn" had Bree assuming her comment had been too much.

"I'm sorry," she whispered. Her voice would've been a whisper even if her throat was at full strength. "That wasn't appropriate."

"No. Don't ever apologize for loving my son with so much fervor. It's the most any mother could ever want for her child. And knowing he feels the same way about you just makes it that much more perfect." She reached down and squeezed Bree's hand where it rested over Tanner's.

"It's still his choice," Bree said. She wanted to make sure he knew he had options.

Mrs. Dempsey nodded. "And we'll make sure he understands that. Tanner always knows his own mind. He knows what he wants. You'll see."

SHE WAS RIGHT there next to him when Tanner opened his eyes the next day.

The doctors assured them it would happen, that he was showing more and more signs of alertness, but until she actually saw those brown eyes looking at her, Bree had not been able to escape the weight that had seemed riveted to her chest.

"Hey, freckles."

And with those two words the weight was gone.

"Hey, hot lips." She reached over and kissed him on them.

He barely made it through talking to his family before falling back asleep, but he was awake again just a couple of hours later. By the next day, he was complaining about the food, and they all knew he was back for good.

Whitaker came by to take Tanner's statement. He was working with the Larimer County Sheriff's Department since so many of the crimes were tied in together. Whitaker asked Bree if she'd be willing to wait outside the hospital room so her testimony wouldn't become tainted by Tanner's version and vice versa. She'd already given her written statement but might have to give one verbally in the future.

Tanner hadn't wanted her to go, but Bree hadn't wanted to relive those details right then anyway.

She'd just gotten Tanner back and awake. She didn't want to think of his still form lying so bloody in her arms again.

She told him she would head to her apartment to take a shower and be back.

While she was there, she looked around. Moving in with Tanner would be such a huge step emotionally, but such a small step physically. It wouldn't take her long to gather up her belongings—after years on the run, she was never going to be a pack rat.

She hadn't been lying to Mrs. Dempsey. There was nothing she wanted more than to be with Tanner. But she only wanted to move in with him if that was what he really wanted, too.

When she got back to the hospital, Whitaker had left, and Cassandra and Mrs. Dempsey were back.

And Tanner was angry.

"What happened?" she croaked, rushing to Tanner's side.

His arms snaked around her hip and pulled her down onto the bed next to him.

Cassandra rolled her eyes. "The big baby is mad because the doctor said he couldn't leave tomorrow. He has to be here at least another day."

"And I told Tanner that I've already got his old room at the house ready for him. I've got my schedule cleared, and I'm ready to wait on him hand and foot as long as he needs me to." Mrs. Dempsey looked pointedly at Bree. "I wanted him to know he has options and can stay wherever he wants."

Bree swallowed the ball of worry in her chest. This was what she'd asked Mrs. Dempsey to do. To make sure he knew he could do what he wanted.

She looked at Tanner. "That all sounds good to me."

His face was scrunched into the most adorable pout she'd ever seen. "First, I don't want to stay in the hospital anymore. The food has not gotten any better since I was here the last time. You would think with all the technological advances our society has made, they could make hospital food more palatable."

She fought not to smile, which was even harder when Cassandra let out a dramatic sigh.

"Just one more day," she whispered to him. "I'll sneak you in food."

"Fine," he said. "But here's the rest. I know it's not fair arguing this with you when your voice doesn't work, but it's the only chance I have against that big brain of yours anyway."

"What are we going to argue about?"

His hand tightened on her hip. "I want you to move in with me."

"Okay," she said instantly. "To help you."

He shook his head. "No, hear me out. I want you to move in with me, not as some sort of nursemaid, although I'm sure I'll need a little help for a couple weeks. I want you to move in with me and stay there. Long after the doctor clears me, I still want you there, waking up with me every morning and going to bed with me every night. This isn't about you being my caregiver or me being your bodyguard. I want you with me, freckles. I love you, and I've wanted you with me from the moment I first saw you shoplifting in that drugstore. If you're not ready, I'll wait. But if you are, there's nothing I want more than having you with me every single day."

She stared at him, heart swelling, not sure she could say anything even if her voice wasn't damaged.

Mrs. Dempsey cleared her throat. When Bree looked over at the older woman, she was grinning. "Looks like he's made his choice."

She nodded and then looked back at Tanner.

"I have made my choice, freckles. And it's you."

"I love you, too," Bree whispered. "And yes, I'll come with you to the ranch."

Tanner's hand slid up her back, pushing her down toward him. His lips pressed against hers gently, mindful of the wounds both of them were recovering from.

Just like the kiss he'd given her at her apartment in Kansas City all those weeks ago, this one was once again full of promise.

Neither of them broke away, even when Cassandra snickered. "I got all of that on camera, and I'm so posting it on YouTube."

Chapter Twenty-Seven

Tanner had honestly never thought he'd wake up again. When he and Bree had fallen to the ground in that bungalow, his last thought was that at least he'd saved her before he'd died.

Nothing had made sense to him as he'd heard her soft voice whispering in his ear while he lay on the floor. No words had penetrated his consciousness, just the knowledge that Bree was there. She was alive. That was enough.

So seeing those green eyes of her staring at him when he'd woken up in the hospital had been a very pleasant surprise. His entire body felt like he'd gone a few rounds with a steamroller, but the look of relief— of love—in Bree's eyes had been worth it.

Talking her into coming here to the ranch? His mother hadn't raised no dummy. And she hadn't tried to hide her approval of Bree coming here to take care of him.

Or her approval of Bree altogether.

And that was a good thing, because he planned to

keep Bree around as long as he could talk her into it. Hopefully forever.

They'd been here three weeks already, and the days hadn't been easy—physically, at least. The road to recovery had taken a lot longer than Tanner had planned. The limitations of his own body as it healed was frustrating. Bed rest was not for him.

That was, until a few days ago, when he'd finally convinced Bree that he was definitely healed enough for her to be in bed with him for more than just sleeping.

After that, *bed rest* hadn't exactly included much *resting.*

Ended up he hadn't needed to take Bree to some fancy resort for their first time making love to be special. The most perfect place on earth had been in his bed at the ranch they both cared so much about.

Maybe their wounds had slowed them down a bit. But that just gave them more of an opportunity to learn everything about each other's bodies.

Not the bed rest the doctor had ordered, but definitely what they'd both needed after coming so close to losing each other.

He watched her now from the rocker on his front porch, coffee cup in hand, as she came walking from the barn. She'd been checking on Star again, as she did at least three times a day. He didn't mind. Like he'd known from the beginning, that pup was helping fill a void in her heart the twins had left.

"Everybody okay in there?"

"Two more weeks until Corfu can start weaning her." Her voice was still a little hoarse but had gotten much better since the attack. And thank God she was finally able to eat solid food. Neither of them wanted to see a smoothie again for the rest of their lives. "I measured Star, and she's definitely right where she should be in terms of size and weight."

Bree had researched enough about dogs over the past three weeks to know more than most vets. Tanner had no doubt that if she said the puppy was developmentally sound, it was true.

Tomorrow was a big day for both of them. Tanner would be back in the office, although he'd be on desk duty for another couple of months until everything healed up more, but still back at the job he loved.

Ryan Fletcher was sitting in a cell, still awaiting indictment. The crimes were complex and closely linked. Definitely three counts of murder—Newkirk, Anders and Duquette—and two counts of attempted murder for him and Bree.

It looked like he would be charged with Glen Carrico's murder, too. Ryan might have saved Bree's life by shooting Glen, but now it looked more like he'd done it to make sure Carrico couldn't tell the truth about what had happened than because of any altruistic impulse on his part to save Bree.

Fletcher had made a deal with Glen. He had agreed to help keep Darin from being transferred to maximum security if Glen took the fall for the murders if anyone came looking. Glen, dying anyway, had agreed.

Fletcher thought he was getting a desperate, witless patsy in Glen. But Glen had been smarter than Fletcher had realized. He'd left a package in a safety-deposit box a day before he died with a letter describing in detail the entire exchange between him and Fletcher. He'd provided plenty of recorded conversations to back up his claim. He'd sent a letter to his brother, explaining that the information was only to be used if Fletcher didn't come through on his promise to keep Darin out of maximum security.

Glen hadn't trusted Fletcher to keep his end of the bargain after he was gone. Smart man.

It was safe to say Fletcher would be spending the rest of his life in prison. The thought didn't bring Tanner any comfort beyond knowing that he and Bree were now safe. Maybe if Tanner had shared his guilt about what had really happened with Nate—all the things he'd wished he'd done differently—instead of keeping his mistakes hidden from Ryan, everything could've turned out differently.

It would never have brought Nate back, but maybe Ryan wouldn't be lost, too.

But one thing bleeding out all over the floor and watching Bree swing from that noose had taught him: every day was a gift. You learn from your mistakes, and you move on—you don't let the past hold you captive.

Bree was learning that, too, in her own way. She

was starting her first computer class for the shelter tomorrow. She'd dropped down to just one or two shifts per week at the Sunrise Diner, Dan and Cheryl more than happy to let her do that, especially once they understood the plan. They were helping at the shelter, too, offering short-order cooking classes and training for anyone who might be interested.

Cassandra and Bree had become fast friends; the two of them already had plans to expand the shelter. He had no doubt it would become a big part of the community.

She walked up the stairs of the porch and wrapped her arms around his waist.

He slipped an arm around her shoulders. "You ready for tomorrow?"

"Yep. Although I'm glad this first class is only for two women. I've already been thinking about some ways I could streamline it and make it more applicable to their lives."

Of course she had been. That didn't surprise him at all. "Oh yeah?"

"I've been doing some research, and I want to make this as effective as possible. These women deserve it."

He kissed the top of her head. "I have no doubt it's going to be the most useful class anyone's ever been a part of, by the time you're done with it."

"How about you? You ready for tomorrow? Ready to go back to being Captain Hot Lips?"

He smiled at the nickname and nodded. He was

more than ready. Ready to be back on the job and doing his part to keep Risk Peak safe.

"Hopefully nobody but you will call me that, but yes, definitely ready. Although being here with you is nothing to scoff at, either."

"I know. It's been nice having some time just the two of us. But the real world will be good, too. What we do is important."

He hugged her more tightly against him. "It is— you're right."

She nodded against his chest and was quiet for a moment. "I've been researching some other important stuff, too."

"Like what?" He took a sip of his coffee and prepared himself for a fifteen-minute one-sided conversation about computer programming in which he would only understand about eight percent of the terms. But he never wanted to make Bree feel like he wasn't interested in what was going on in that giant brain of hers, even if he didn't always understand it.

"Reverse cowgirl," she said.

He spewed the coffee out over her head. "What?" he croaked.

"Reverse cowgirl." She leaned back so she could look in his eyes. "It's a sexual position where—"

"I know what it is." His voice was still choked. He could not even imagine what she meant when she said she'd been *researching* it.

She nodded solemnly. "I think I would like to try it."

He swallowed a laugh and kissed her. *This woman.* She was going to keep him on his toes for the next sixty years or so.

And he couldn't wait.

* * * * *

Look for the next book in USA TODAY *bestselling author Janie Crouch's miniseries* The Risk Series: A Bree and Tanner Thriller *when* Constant Risk *goes on sale in September.*

And don't miss the previous title in the series:

Calculated Risk

Available now from Harlequin Intrigue!

COMING NEXT MONTH FROM
⊞ HARLEQUIN®

INTRIGUE

Available August 20, 2019

#1875 TANGLED THREAT
by Heather Graham

Years ago, FBI agent Brock McGovern was arrested for a crime he didn't commit. Now that he's been cleared of all charges, he'll do whatever it takes to find the culprit. With two women missing, Brock's ex-girlfriend Maura Antrium is eager to help him. Can they find the killer...or will he find them first?

#1876 FULL FORCE
Declan's Defenders • by Elle James

After working at the Russian embassy in Washington, DC, Emily Chastain is targeted by a relentless killer. When she calls upon Declan's Defenders in order to find someone to help her, former Force Recon marine Frank "Mustang" Ford vows to find the person who is threatening her.

#1877 THE SAFEST LIES
A Winchester, Tennessee Thriller • by Debra Webb

Special Agent Sadie Buchanen is deep in the backcountry of Winchester, Tennessee, in order to retrieve a hostage taken by a group of extreme survivalists. When she finds herself in danger, she must rely on Smith Flynn, an intriguing stranger who is secretly an undercover ATF special agent.

#1878 MURDERED IN CONARD COUNTY
Conard County: The Next Generation • by Rachel Lee

When a man is killed, Blaire Afton and Gus Maddox, two park rangers, must team up to find the murderer. Suddenly, they discover they are after a serial killer... But can they stop him before he claims another victim?

#1879 CONSTANT RISK
The Risk Series: A Bree and Tanner Thriller • by Janie Crouch

A serial killer is loose in Dallas, and only Bree Daniels and Tanner Dempsey can stop him. With bodies piling up around them, can they find the murderer before more women die?

#1880 WANTED BY THE MARSHAL
American Armor • by Ryshia Kennie

After nurse Kiera Connell is abducted by a serial killer and barely escapes with her life, she must rely on US marshal Travis Johnson's protection. But while Travis believes the murderer is in jail, Kiera knows a second criminal is on the loose and eager to silence her.

YOU CAN FIND MORE INFORMATION ON UPCOMING HARLEQUIN® TITLES, FREE EXCERPTS AND MORE AT WWW.HARLEQUIN.COM.

HICNM0819

"I've been assigned to go back to Florida. To stay at the Frampton Ranch and Resort—and investigate what we believe to be three kidnappings and a murder. And the kidnappings may have nothing to do with the resort, nor may the murder?" Brock McGovern asked, a small note of incredulity slipping into his voice, which was surprising to him—he was always careful to keep an even tone.

FBI assistant director Richard Egan had brought him into his office, and Brock had known he was going on assignment—he just hadn't expected this.

"Yes, not what you'd want, but, hey, maybe it'll be good for you—and perhaps necessary now, when time is of the essence and there is no one out there who could know the place or the circumstances with the same scope and experience you have," Egan told him. "Three young women have disappeared from the area. Two of them were guests of the Frampton Ranch and Resort shortly before their disappearances—the third had left St. Augustine and was on her way there. The Florida Department of Law Enforcement has naturally been there already. They asked for federal help on this. Shades of the past haunt them—they don't want any more unsolved murders—and everyone is hoping against hope that Lily Sylvester, Amy Bonham and Lydia Merkel might be found."

"These are Florida missing-person cases," Brock said. "And it's sad but true that young people go to Florida and get caught up in the beach life and the club scene. And regrettable but true once again—there's a drug and alcohol culture that does exist and people get caught up in it. Not just in Florida, of course, but everywhere." He smiled grimly. "I go where I'm told, but I'm curious—how is this an FBI affair? And forgive me, but—FBI out of New York?"

"Not out of New York. FDLE asked for you. Specifically."

Don't miss
Tangled Threat *by Heather Graham,*
available September 2019 wherever
Harlequin® books and ebooks are sold.

www.Harlequin.com

HIEXP0819